THE IMPERSONAL ADVENTURE

MARCEL BÉALU

THE IMPERSONAL ADVENTURE

TRANSLATED BY GEORGE MACLENNAN

WAKEFIELD PRESS

CAMBRIDGE, MASSACHUSETTS

Wakefield Press, P.O. Box 425645, Cambridge, MA 02142

Originally published as *L'Aventure impersonelle* by Arcanes in 1954.
© Editions Phébus, Paris, 1985

This book was set in Garamond Premier Pro and Helvetica Neue Pro by Wakefield Press. Printed and bound by McNaughton & Gunn, Inc., in the United States of America.

ISBN: 978-1-939663-72-6

Available through D.A.P./Distributed Art Publishers
75 Broad Street, Suite 630
New York, New York 10004
Tel: (212) 627-1999
Fax: (212) 627-9484

10   9   8   7   6   5   4   3   2   1

REFERENCE POINTS

TRANSLATOR'S INTRODUCTION

Marcel Béalu enjoys a following in the English-speaking world, albeit a limited one, thanks to a translation of his novel *The Experience of the Night*, as well as "The Water Spider," the story for which he is best known in his native France.[1] These are prominent among the writings that once saw him described, to his great chagrin, as "the Pope of the fantastic." His activities, however, extended well beyond the literature of the strange. He also made his mark as a poet, a bookseller, the editor of a journal, an anthologist (including an anthology of erotic poetry), and a memoirist. As an amateur artist he devoted time to drawing and painting.

Not all his fiction can be classified as fantastic; Béalu disliked repeating himself, and in his novels he explored other avenues, including realism, autobiographical fiction, and utopian fiction.[2] However, it would be fair to say that in his native France as elsewhere he is best known as a writer of the fantastic, with his most distinctive works lying within this territory.

The Impersonal Adventure stands alongside *The Experience of the Night* as his most extended exercise in the genre. The two books, however, are different from each other in significant respects; whereas *The Experience of the Night* chronicles the strange adventures of the protagonist in a dreamlike wonderland, *The Impersonal Adventure* unfolds in a more realistically situated urban milieu and tells a more compact story framed by a conventional narrative structure—that of the quest narrative. Nevertheless, Béalu's imagination was working at full stretch in *The Adventure*; none of his subsequent long-form works of fiction measure up to this and *The Experience of the Night* in terms of fresh imaginative invention.

*

Ogyges, a huge and heterogeneously diverse retail empire, is a central presence in *The Impersonal Adventure*. It's hardly a coincidence that Béalu's own story is largely taken up by retail. He was born in 1908 to parents who ran a hat shop in Saumur; his earliest memories included playing behind the counter. The milieu was petit bourgeois, but family circumstances were straitened, with little money to spare. Béalu's formal education ended at the age of twelve when he went to work to help support his parents. Eventually he was apprenticed to a hatter and learned the artisanal skills of the trade. From there he proceeded, at age seventeen, to work in a Parisian hat shop. It was at this time that he met Marguerite Kessel (also known as Daisy), a mature and attractive German woman residing in the same hotel. The teenage Béalu (a good-looking youth, it should be said) became her favored suitor; thirteen years his senior, she eventually became his first wife.[3]

In 1931, following a spell in national service, he assumed responsibility for the family hat shop, now named Chapellerie Marcel, located in the town of Montargis some seventy-five miles from Paris. Here he met and became friendly with Henri Lefebvre.[4] Lefebvre, working at that time in Montargis as a schoolteacher, had already established himself as a Marxist theorist and philosopher. In initial sympathy with both Dadaism and surrealism, Lefebvre had contacts with Tristan Tzara and André Breton, among others. His literary and avant-garde connections were to prove important for Béalu, who was indebted to him for an introduction, in 1937, to Max Jacob, who at that point had converted to Catholicism and was residing at the nearby abbey of Saint-Benoît-sur-Loire. Over the following seven years Jacob became an important figure in Béalu's life: friend, mentor, and literary father-figure. "He taught me to write," Béalu would later claim.[5]

After a period in uniform in 1939–1940 (he saw no action), Béalu was once more behind the counter in Montargis for the duration of the Occupation, selling hats. Not for nothing do the three volumes of his memoirs carry the overall title *Le chapeau magique* (The magic hat).

The shopkeeper wasn't untouched by the war; his business required late-night train journeys to Paris, always at risk of being bombed. Events touched him personally when Max Jacob was arrested as a Jew and interned in Drancy, scheduled to be transferred to Auschwitz. Béalu was one of those who tried to rescue him, contacting Jean Cocteau who, through his connections, managed to secure a safe passage for the poet. But it was too late: Jacob died of bronchial pneumonia before he could be released. Béalu felt the loss deeply.

Béalu discovered poetry and literature only after leaving school. An initial, enthralling encounter with Lamartine's verse (via the medium of a cinema screen) set him on a course of reading, writing, and self-education that effectively changed the course of his life. Although he developed a particular passion for poetry, his first published writings

to make a mark were idealistic essays preaching a gospel of human-
ist anarchism and pacifism. These earned him the recognition of Jean
Giono and Élie Faure, among others; however, his meeting with Max
Jacob soon pointed him in a more purely literary direction: "When,"
Jacob asked, "will you stop wasting your time with this parish-pump
journalism to become the grand poet that you are?"[6] Béalu found his
own voice at the end of the 1930s when his first important creative
writings were published, but he never escaped "le souci du bifteck"[7]—
the need earn enough to put bread on the table. His memoirs give an
account of the composition of *The Experience of the Night*:

> It was written between 1942 and 1943 in the room above the hat
> shop at 21, Rue Dorée, Montargis . . . filling some pages every
> morning and evening, before and after shop hours, when, dis-
> guised as a shopkeeper, I advised men, women, and children on
> the purchase of a cap, a soft felt hat, a lady's bonnet with flow-
> ers, or a sailor's beret.[8]

"Never renounce hats. They'll belong to your legend." Such was Max
Jacob's advice to Béalu,[9] and one can envisage an account of Béalu's
life written up in the manner of Marcel Schwob's *Imaginary Lives*: the
hatter and shopkeeper become poet of dreams. In 1944, however, with
his first signature work, *Mémoires de l'ombre* (Memories of darkness)
published by the prestigious firm of Gallimard,[10] and *The Experience
of the Night* scheduled for publication, Béalu was eager to devote himself more exclusively to writing:

> The apartment above the Montargis hatshop was full of books
> that, for me, represented freedom. *Vases communicants*:[11] I'd
> acquire freedom on the day that I was able to live entirely among

books. The solution—the compromise—consisted in exchanging hats for books. But I still had no idea of becoming a bookseller.[12]

Instead, selling off the Montargis hat shop, he purchased a splendid if somewhat dilapidated house in Fontainebleau. But financial concerns soon pressed in: "I tried to establish a second-hand goods shop on the ground floor. It was madness in a district where there was no footfall. Over six months, two eventual clients opened my door."[13] We might well guess that the Ogyges retail empire that figures in *The Impersonal Adventure*, with its deserted premises, devoid of customers and full of unsold goods, is a nightmare projection of the Fontainebleau shop. It was in fact during this period that the seeds of *The Impersonal Adventure* were planted: Béalu tells us that the account of the demented auction of goods that occurs in Part IV of the book derived from his experience of haunting sales rooms at this time. If the dates that he gives for the composition of the work (1945–1949) are to be trusted,[14] then *The Impersonal Adventure* is the confused, anxiety-laden nightmare that the writer produced during a period of particular uncertainty; having given up the hat shop, he was buying and selling houses, trying to make his way as a writer, and struggling to gain a sufficient income.

Through the 1940s, Béalu bought and sold books on a casual basis. The separate threads of trade and literature fully intertwined when, in 1950, he moved to Paris and opened a second-hand bookshop. This venture was more in tune with his creative avocation than the selling of hats or used goods, and he was happy enough to continue life as a bookseller, which he did for the next forty or so years: "I would certainly have preferred to devote myself entirely to literature. Would I have written better? I don't think so. . . . When it becomes urgent to say something one always finds the time."[15] The second volume of his memoirs, covering the bookshop years, is entitled *Porte ouverte sur la rue* (Door open on the street). Béalu, it might be said, held court here; a number of distinguished visitors came through the door, whether to buy books or specifically to meet him. Among others, he mentions Jacques Lacan, André Breton, Max Ernst, René Magritte, Jacques Prévert, and René Char. Here, late in life, he met his third wife, a young student named Josée.

Though the location of the premises changed from time to time, Béalu's name for the bookshop remained constant and was to become well known in Parisian literary circles: Le Pont Traversé (The crossed bridge). It was named after a story by Jean Paulhan, and the title was perhaps in Béalu's mind when he was writing *The Impersonal Adventure*: the crossing of a bridge leads Fidibus, the narrator, to the unnamed island where his adventure unfolds.

*

Béalu, who commented readily on his other major works of fiction, had surprisingly little to say about *The Impersonal Adventure*. He's not alone in this. The work was largely ignored on publication and hasn't gained a great deal of attention since. However, its general neglect by the literary world was compensated elsewhere; it gained a distinguished admirer in the person of René Magritte, who wrote to Béalu in 1954:

> I've read *L'Aventure impersonnelle*, very much regretting that the book had to finish. I experienced the same lost pleasure that I had in 1913 or thereabouts with Fantomas. Fidibus, Torve [Squint], Morve [Snot], and Muta are companions who don't let boredom gain the upper hand. But, enjoyment aside, this hostile and mediocre world that reduces us to nothing very much

is transformed by the subterranean light whose secret you possess.[16]

If Béalu's "secret" produces any light at all, it's certainly of a subterranean nature. Fidibus's narrative commences with a reference to a notebook that serves as aide-memoire—but one that is flawed by lapses into illegibility. As we read on, we learn that gaps in the record extend further; Fidibus has blanked out the memory of a previous visit to the island, one involving a memorable sexual encounter. If our narrator isn't unreliable, then he's certainly problematic; his voice too, particularly in the opening chapters, is sometimes allusive and sometimes quirkily stylized. The reader learns nothing about where Fidibus has come from or where he might go to, learns in fact very little about his person: we aren't even told his true name. He also cuts a poor figure as a quester-hero, usually at the mercy of events rather than in control of them. Taking all this into account, the first-person narrative can be seen as an inverted memoir—a memory of darkness, to borrow the title of one of Béalu's most celebrated works (*Mémoires de l'ombre*).

The problems aren't limited to the narrator; conversations between characters are often elliptical, involving speculations and implications that remain opaque. Backstories that should throw light on characters and situations are multiplied with no one version finally confirmed as definitive. The barriers between what is real, what is delirious, and what is fabulous in the narrative become porous and unreliable.

Magritte's 1954 letter to Béalu continues:

The questioner that I am and that I believe you are, too, find ourselves enriched—through what you throw light on—with an IDEA which I would express thus: we are straying along a straight road—along the *only* possible road—as a reply to our questions.[17]

"Nous errons dans un droit chemin" (We are straying along a straight road); the phrase might also be translated as "We are astray on a straight road." In this version it bears some resemblance to an image that emerges in Part IV of the novella. In a chapter entitled "Spinners of Events," Fidibus comes upon two ancient ladies engaged in lacework. "Where are we?" he asks.

> Graciously, but in a croaking voice, the old woman who seemed absorbed in the production of the fine lace, putting her spindles aside, replies, *Come here young man, don't be afraid* . . . (and placing her wrinkled finger on an imperceptible point of the work spread out in front of her). *Look . . . we're there.* I then understand that these networks of numberless stitches are the map of the island.

The retail empire that plays a central role in the novella takes its name from its founder, a certain Ogyges. The name is reminiscent of Ogygia, the island where, in Homer's *Odyssey*, the nymph Calypso, in love with Odysseus, holds him as her reluctant guest:

> Upon her hearthstone a great fire blazing
> Scented the farthest shores with cedar smoke
> and smoke of thyme, and singing high and low
> in her sweet voice, before her loom a-weaving,
> she passed her golden shuttle to and fro.[18]

The two ancient spinners of the Administrative Council might be seen as Calypso's descendants, and the island, for all its appearance of urban modernity—hotel, houses, café, shops, emporiums—is a place through which mythical and magical currents flow. No one works for a living here; no economically productive work is done at all. In the Ogyges shops, commodity capitalism has become a hollow, meaningless shell: nothing is bought, nothing is sold; the contents of the shops and warehouses are finally dispersed or destroyed in a grotesque and carnivalesque auction of goods. Names—Fidibus, Snot, Muta (mute, mutable, transmutation)—are animistically related to persons. Time is deliriously dilated or else impossibly accelerated, as when the young woman Corinne's pregnancy develops to nearly full term in a mere day or two. The space of the island is no less heterodox; the map created by the spinners' lacework is linked "through impalpable correspondences" to the space it represents: when it's reduced to ashes along with the two spinners, the fate of the island itself is prefigured. Space then becomes nightmarishly elongated for Fidibus when he runs in hot pursuit of the heavily pregnant Corinne but is never able to catch up with her.

At the conclusion, Fidibus remains bewildered by the mysteries and anomalies he has encountered, and the reader likewise. The questions asked in the story are those that we might also wish to ask: "Who are you Fidibus? You aren't Fidibus, you aren't a representative! Who are you?" No answer is forthcoming. "*You can be sure of finding what you're looking for there*" is the advice given by a friend at the start of the story, but what exactly is Fidibus is looking for? We never find out. Magritte was right to suggest that a darker, subterranean light is shining behind the dime novel apparatus of mystery. *The Impersonal Adventure* is a work that provokes as much as it entertains the reader. An afterword appended at the end of this translation will explore that provocation further in an attempt to throw more light on proceedings.

*

For all its unanswered questions and occasional stylistic quirks, *The Impersonal Adventure* is, on the whole, written in clear, idiomatic prose. Events are sharply drawn, and the story is shaped toward a definite conclusion. Tantalizing anomalies are also offset by the pace of events, which becomes increasingly rapid as the novella progresses toward its denouement. With its relative brevity, it's a quick read and, for those attuned to strange fiction, an absorbing one.

This sense of pace is facilitated by aspects of the novella's composition and structure that deserve comment.

Fidibus speaks in the present tense, which results in a strong sense of immediacy. Encounters and impressions are registered in a manner that's faintly reminiscent of the stream of consciousness novel. Although, as narrator, he's able to reflect on the people he meets and the situations in which he is involved, first impressions sometimes have to be revised or corrected in light of ongoing developments ("I understand my mistake"). There is no sense of the resolved retrospect that a past tense narrative would imply, something that corresponds to our hero's lack of a lived past. He is carried forward to an undetermined future by the rapid current of the present tense.

Béalu's narrative also creates some abrupt and rapid transitions, akin to cinematic jump cuts:

> Every interruption of habit strengthens that seriousness which enables us to judge how futile are our occupations. A rolling stone gathers no moss, but it acquires the smoothness and polish that any honest stone should aspire to. My room is wedged between leprous walls, overlooking a courtyard, all of whose windows are closed. The hotel manager stares at me in amazement when I let him know that I plan on having supper.

Such jolting gear changes signal the compressed nature of the narrative, but they also occur because there are no paragraph divisions in the entire text of *The Impersonal Adventure*. The book is divided into four numbered parts, and, within these, into a quantity of brief sections. Each section is a block of prose not only without paragraphs but also without lines breaks for direct speech—in fact with no line breaks at all. Each section also bears its own title, with the titles listed separately in a contents page. Wakefield editor Marc Lowenthal points out the unorthodoxy of this page. In the 1954 first edition, chapter titles are conventionally listed as "Table des matières"—i.e., list of contents, but in the definitive 1985 Phébus edition, "Table des matières" becomes instead "Repères," i.e., reference points, as though the section titles were grid listings. These titled sections aren't conventionally set out as chapters, being merely separated from each other by white spaces, This procedure repeats that of the earlier novel, *L'Expérience de la nuit*, though not, it should be said, in the Dedalus English translation, which interferes with Béalu's formal arrangement by joining the blocks of prose together as paragraphs—a betrayal of the French text. "This book," Béalu stated apropos of *L'Expérience*, "was a poem for me; four sections, each one composed of stanzas separated by a white space."[19] The specification of section titles as "reference points" in *The Impersonal Adventure* arguably hints in its turn at a certain kinship with poetry; as envisaged by Béalu, the text is a space to be traversed as much as a narrative unfolding in time. *The Impersonal Adventure*, it has to be said, is clearly the work of a novelist, but both formally and in the enigmas it presents, it also remains the work of a poet.

NOTES

1. *The Experience of the Night*, trans. Christine Donougher (Cambs: Dedalus, 1997). "The Water Spider" has been translated twice, by Michael Bullock and Edward Gauvin, respectively.

2. See, respectively, *La Millanderie* (1949), *Passage de la bête* (1969), and *La Poudre des songes* (1977).

3. As time went on, Marguerite became intensely and (as Béalu would have it) irrationally jealous. In 1951, the relationship finally broke down under the strain.

4. Looking back on Lefebvre in his memoirs some fifty years later, when the two had long since lost contact, Béalu seemed somewhat bemused by his former friend's Marxian theorizing and more inclined to notice his serial womanizing. However, he noted one of Lefebvre's major works, *The Critique of Everyday Life*, which he must have looked into—it includes a critical discussion of the nineteenth- and twentieth-century literature of the weird, from Baudelaire to the surrealists.

5. Marcel Béalu, *Le Regard oblique: Entretiens avec Marie-France Azar* (Paris: Jean-Michel Laplace, 1993), 50.

6. Marcel Béalu, *Enfances et apprentissage* (Paris: Belfond, 1980), 198.

7. Marcel Béalu, *Porte ouverte sur la rue* (Paris: Belfond, 1981), 94.

8. *Porte ouverte sur la rue*, 39–40.

9. *Porte ouverte sur la rue*, 59.

10. The 1944 Gallimard edition comprised a total of 74 short prose *récits*; the definitive edition published by Le Terrain Vague in 1959 added a further 45 pieces. In *Présent définitif* (1983), the final volume of his memoirs,

Béalu noted that Michael Bullock was working on an English translation, but this, if completed, never saw the light of day.

11. *Vases communicants*, literally "communicating vessels," though the expression, a common one in French, lacks a convenient English equivalent. It's generally understood to mean spillover or interconnection between two entities—in this case, books and freedom.

12. *Porte ouverte sur la rue*, 10.

13. *Porte ouverte sur la rue*, 60.

14. But are these dates to be trusted? *Porte sur la rue* provides a detailed account of Béalu's writing and editorial activities between 1945 and 1948; these include *Journal d'un mort* (1947), "L'Araignée d'eau" (1948), his realist novel *La Millanderie* (1948), an anthology of erotic poetry, and some journalistic writings. Add to that the vicissitudes of moving houses twice, trying to run a shop, and trading in books on the side, and there wouldn't seem to be much room left for writing *The Impersonal Adventure*. It's noteworthy that the only reference to the birth of the work during this difficult time is to its conception and not its composition: "the conception of this story certainly came to me during this period" (*Porte ouverte*, 61). If the seeds of the novella were planted in 1945–1946, it might have been written in 1949, but Béalu's near silence on the writing of the work remains puzzling, and it's possible that the composition in fact belongs to the early 1950s.

15. *Porte ouverte sur la rue*, 138–139.

16. In *Porte ouverte sur la rue*, 211.

17. In *Porte ouverte sur la rue*, 211.

18. *The Odyssey*, trans. Robert Fitzgerald (London: Heinemann, 1961), 75.

19. Béalu, *Le Regard oblique*, 61.

THE IMPERSONAL ADVENTURE

Captain Delano crossed over to him, and stood in silence surveying the knot; his mind, by a not uncongenial transition, passing from its own entanglements to those of the hemp. For intricacy such a knot he had never seen in an American ship, or indeed any other. The old man looked like an Egyptian priest, making Gordian knots for the temple of Ammon. The knot seemed a combination of double-bowline-knot, treble-crown-knot, back-handed-well-knot, knot-in-and-out-knot, and jamming-knot.

At last, puzzled to comprehend the meaning of such a knot, Captain Delano addressed the knotter:—

"What are you knotting there, my man?"

"The knot," was the brief reply, without looking up.

"So it seems; but what is it for?"

"For someone else to undo," muttered back the old man, plying his fingers harder than ever, the knot being now nearly completed.

While Captain Delano stood watching him, suddenly the old man threw the knot toward him, and said in broken English,—the first heard in the ship,—something to this effect—"Undo it, cut it, quick." It was said lowly, but with such condensation of rapidity, that the long, slow words in Spanish, which had preceded and followed, almost operated as covers to the brief English between.

For a moment, knot in hand, and knot in head, Captain Delano stood mute; while, without further heeding him, the old man was now intent upon other ropes. Presently there was a slight stir behind Captain Delano. Turning, he saw the chained Negro, Atufal, standing quietly there. The next moment the old sailor rose, muttering, and, followed by his subordinate Negroes, removed to the forward part of the ship, where in the crowd he disappeared.

An elderly Negro, in a clout like an infant's, and with a pepper and salt head, and a kind of attorney air, now approached Captain Delano. In tolerable Spanish, and with a good-natured, knowing wink, he informed him that the old knotter was simple-witted, but harmless; often playing his old tricks.

H. Melville, *Benito Cereno*

I

Having concluded the business that brought me to A...
there's nothing more to keep me in this city, but neither
is there any pressing need for me to move on to another. Rare are the moments when we feel ourselves once
more at liberty. In that holiday mood, leafing through
the notebook I use for memoranda, I find a half-erased
name and address. And I suddenly remember the advice of a friend whom I've since lost sight of: *If you ever
happen to go to A..., be sure to visit Og... Og...s* (the
name is completely illegible), *you'll find what you're looking for there.* But I can't even remember the reason for
the advice, it was all so long ago. What could I have
wanted back then in a city where I never thought I'd
find myself? That lapse in memory goads my curiosity. Deploring the carelessness that all too often makes
me scribble notes in pencil, a sure guarantee of their
impermanence, I immediately enquire about Rue des
Carmes or Rue des Larmes ... Impossible to make out
what exactly the first letter is! There's a long pause before

the hotelier ventures an opinion, and I'm on the point of abandoning my enquiry, not liking to bother others with matters that concern only myself. As I turn my back, though, the man suddenly says, *Wait . . . Maybe it's Rue des Charmes?* (Noticing an odd change of expression on the hotelier's face, I feel obliged to add, with a show of unconcern, for my face has turned crimson and I start to babble): *Of course! It's not entirely impossible . . . in fact . . . maybe . . . yes indeed.* I finally get some vague directions, but, while speaking, the hotelier stares at me so insistently that, agitated, I only retain some of them. In the street I immediately think to make a note of these pointers, but this time I don't even have the damned pencil stub! Such tiny oversights and the automatic gestures, the evasive responses that accompany them, due more to my poor emotional self-control than to actual carelessness, often earn me a reputation for empty-headedness among my closest friends. Don't they in fact see me as someone with his head in the clouds? Head in the clouds! . . . If the directions have now completely slipped my mind, it's because I'm gripped by a new concern, namely the fixed idea of finding different accommodations for the few days that I still plan on spending here. Certainly, this decision isn't unrelated to the look that the hotelier gave me. His reply must, however, have impressed itself sufficiently on my mind to affect my wandering footsteps. He probably hinted, in the muddled way in which so-called simple souls like to express their thoughts, *You*

MARCEL BÉALU

have to get there by boat . . . because it's to the river that I'm led by my search for new lodgings.

In addition to the instinct that drives him to preserve his anonymity by surrounding himself with precautions, the solitary man is drawn to the unknown, even if it proves sordid. But were he to attain the total freedom of which he dreams, it would soon be transformed into a forest of fear. On these pavements, in the slight fog rising from the river, it's seemingly only the familiar faces of housewives or low-grade employees that pass me by, seeing me as one of their own. The district that the inhabitants of A . . . call "the island" remains linked to their suburbs and settlements on the other bank by means of two long suspension bridges with planking so worm-eaten that vehicles no longer dare undertake the crossing. But it's an abandoned district; it could even more accurately be called *condemned*. Those people whose incurable restlessness drives them to frequent movement take the big reinforced concrete bridge a few kilometers upstream that directly spans the two banks of the river. Newly arrived in these surroundings, I hesitate for several minutes on seeing in the distance an assemblage of old buildings the color of moss, rust, and coal, surrounded by stagnant water, like an enormous steamer with no masts. A few hideous constructions like those that overhang housing projects emerge from that conglomeration; their ill-defined purpose has varied so many times, even over the course of their erection, that they harbor an ambiguous air of dilapidation and incompletion. It's hard to imagine that, for centuries, extensive parks in these same places sheltered marvelous châteaux. Velledas or the Apollo decapitated by a laughing warrior are currently flaking away between the bricks of building lots.[1] But even if cities, just like lives, get worn out, even if it isn't only the alluring odors of young bodies that go sour, the gods aren't so quick to die. After crossing the swaying bridge, my attention is caught by two words traced in enormous imitation gold letters at the foot of a frightful building with a faux marble plinth:

HOTEL PROVIDENCE

Under New Management is painted underneath in letters that are rain-smudged but still readable, on a banner that's torn by the wind that blows continually down that avenue like a corridor between the bridges. I'm not at all surprised that probably no one has noticed the sublime irony of those two inscriptions. Perhaps that's the cause, in raising my thoughts to the kind of luminosity that makes them liable to frolic high above common contingencies, of a little incident that will subsequently prove consequential. It strikes me as amusing to sign the manager's register with an invented name: *Fidibus*. Confronted with the entry for *Profession*, I feel somewhat

MARCEL BÉALU

abashed. Which to choose from the many jobs in my life? Isn't it scandalous that, at over thirty-five years of age, a man should be so utterly without a career? That he hasn't yet *dug his hole* in the field of individual endeavors (an expression that I'm very fond of on account of the hole in the earth, everyone's final destination)[2] can only indicate his utter lack of capacity. Finally, succumbing to a whim of the moment, I write in my best hand, *Representative*. A designation that always makes me laugh. Representative of what? The devil alone would be able to tell you.

Providing myself so easily with a new identity has put me in a good mood. It's all about making a success of your first steps Fidibus! ... Why has this word—the name of a paper spill[3]—rather than another come to mind? A mystery. And, having become an ember, to which fire should I apply my flame? Through these inconsequential reflections a part of the game suppressed until now is suggested to me. The truth is that I'm pleased to have made a decision and put it into effect so quickly. Every interruption of habit strengthens that seriousness which enables us to judge how futile are our occupations. A rolling stone gathers no moss, but it acquires the smoothness and polish that any honest stone should aspire to. My room is wedged between leprous walls, overlooking a courtyard, all of whose windows are closed. The hotel manager stares at me in amazement when I let him know that I plan on having supper. Finally, he sees fit to direct me to a café for that purpose: the Café du Printemps, in the lower part of the island. I must be thankful for a room at the Hotel Providence, an exceptional favor conceded to rare passing customers. I'm even, he assures me, the only one of those odd characters to have been seen in quite a while. The establishment will soon be put on the market, and all its rooms—excepting mine—are already pretty well redundant, along with the kitchens. Not wishing at the moment to hurry off in search of that cheap eatery, I take a seat in the empty dining room after having begged the waiter to serve me sandwiches and a drink. There, to keep up appearances, I unfold a news-paper kept for wrapping up some object or other. But impossible to follow a line of it, so unfamiliar have the problems of the day and their jargon become, as distant as the *Lex Ripuaria* or that of the Burgraves. Passing over the reception of the world boxing champion at the Municipal Coliseum by the leading lights of Science, the Navy, and the Republic, my eyes stray to the second page where an editor, no doubt with a college diploma, opines sanctimoniously on contemporary humanism, progres-sive materialism, the new world, and I don't know what else, when a word flung from the entrance abruptly cap-tures my attention. In front of the waiter, who is noncha-lantly wiping glasses, a customer, who is very concerned with keeping an eye on the street, confronts a species

MARCEL BÉALU

of shabby, unshaven beggar. I thought I heard *Rue des Charmes* . . . Soon, the chatter of two such dissimilar men intrigues me for another reason; underneath a feigned indifference they are deeply engrossed, as though using a coded language aimed at fooling indiscreet ears. That impression is troubling and I'm relieved when the grimy, beggarly looking little man slips away, making way for a young woman, probably the person for whom the other man, visibly impatient, hasn't stopped watching. At this change of personnel, and noting the "charm" of the new-comer, I understand my mistake. Keyed up with waiting, the customer at the counter just now was simply evoking these very "charms." A heated discussion ensues between the man and the young woman, but it's voiced so low that I still can't catch anything, and all I can do to satisfy a sudden and now very lively curiosity is to try to get a glimpse of their faces. Pallid, seemingly prickly, the man prompts suspicions of secretive calculations and an un-wholesome brutality. His extreme nervousness is evident, betrayed too by the harsh and dull sound of his voice. Beside him, the young woman's naïve and sweet face, a pink tulip in bloom, reveals a transparently unquiet soul; these ingenuous petals disclose wounded pride, indigna-tion, suffering, but, equally, an inflexible will. Yes, the of-ten invisible abyss that separates people yawns open here, unfathomable.

The dialogue is promptly cut short when I get to my feet, something that, in spite of the disagreement, indicates a degree of complicity. I'm gripped by a desire to, at all costs, meet again that young woman whose existence was unknown to me until only a few minutes ago, as though it's within my power to save her from adversity. It's an odd quirk of mine that I can only ever imagine a young woman as being in some kind of danger, therefore in need of rescue (no doubt in the secret hope of then becoming the object of her gratitude). But after pacing the length of the avenue several times, I abandon my quest and my illusions. *Damned gallant heart*, I mutter, *always ready to swallow the same bait!* I head slowly toward the center of the island, not without looking back every second, for I still can't believe that such an uplifting hope is in vain. I'm about to carry on toward the lower regions of the island when a klaxon sounds, at length. Immediately I'm engulfed in a flood of people of all different types and ages and who seem to emerge from the ground, climbing, rushing, toward the main avenue. This throng is cloaked in an infinite weariness like a halo of dust. In order to resist the current, I retrace my steps toward the bridge, reaching it with some difficulty and a strong desire at that moment to return to my previous haunts on the other bank of the river. I'm stunned not just by the despondency, the shabby looks, the greed of all these faces, but also by their sullenness and their sometimes ill-natured obstinacy. A fresh roar makes itself heard, and, turning round, I can't see a living soul. At that moment, hurried steps at the far end of the avenue catch my attention. The young woman so impatiently awaited a few moments ago hastens toward me. Seized yet again by that hope which is the instinct of fatality I fling myself in her direction. We rush toward each other, but I'm the only one of us who knows it. We're barely ten meters apart when, swerving, she vanishes into one of the shops. It's a huge emporium of "Furniture, Used Goods, Curios" where everything necessary for furnishing the home is on sale, old and new all jumbled together. Various interiors are simulated by the numerous displays, so effectively that they might be called true "slices of life," like those automobiles that show, in section, their most secret mechanical parts. Dining rooms, living rooms, bedrooms, boudoirs, studios, bathrooms, all arranged with meticulous detail, convey to perfection an idea of lived-in apartments. The illusion is completed by some mannequins placed here and there in poses that, for all their conventionality, differ hardly at all from those that a camera lens would capture in the intimacy of a domestic interior. From the outside, I have to search among these motionless silhouettes before recognizing the young woman, and when, taking care not to show myself, I'm finally able to observe her, I'm taken aback by her odd behavior. First she put down her handbag, took off her gloves, removed her hat and light overcoat, but instead of hanging them from a peg as I was expecting, she now strips off her pullover, her skirt and, hastily, with the help of those items of clothing, topped off by a mask that she takes from a drawer, she sets up a kind of crude replica of herself on the empty chair behind the desk, intended in all likelihood to mimic her presence. Precaution thus taken, and after looking around several times, she disappears, a scantily clad nymph, into the depths of the shop.

For a long time, I remain with nose pressed to the glass, prey to strange thoughts. My feeling of disquiet is in no way diminished by the walk with which I then pass the time. The Hotel Providence, if I'm its solitary guest, is the only establishment of this kind on the island. The commercial sector where I've thoughtlessly taken up residence consists entirely of shops identical to the one I've just been observing, all of them bearing just these words on their facades: *Furniture, Used Goods, Curios*. The repetition of this last term eventually irritates me, for the fact is that I can hardly see any *curios*. Everywhere, unfailingly, examples of "interiors" always admirably arranged, but deserted, as though abandoned. For I'm no longer fooled by purely decorative mannequins. Where are the managers, sales staff, cashiers, directors? Has the bustling herd of a short while ago left behind nothing but a scattering of these ludicrous semblances, the likes of which I've just seen with the young woman? Only

MARCEL BÉALU

nearsighted customers would be fooled by them. But do customers still venture into the district? Perhaps the sole purpose of all these window displays, also purely decorative, is to mislead restless spirits like myself. Aren't I alone in roaming these empty streets where, in any event, I've only set foot as a passerby, a dilettante, and not at all as a prospective buyer? Fleeing this wilderness of shops infested with failure, I trudge through a tangle of little streets that intersect and diverge in indeterminate routes, through building lots and waste ground, until it's time to eat. One after another dissimilar houses succeed each other, all devoid of inhabitants. Through gaping windows, I see dirty, disordered, miserably furnished dwellings, and I'm struck by the contrast between these hovels and the spotlessness of the window displays. But, little by little, they fill up with familiar sounds: the clinking of tableware, the sizzle of the dish heating up on the stove, the squalling of children around the table, a cacophony of radios. A vast racket that is penetrated by the full-throated and happy laugh of a woman, illuminated by the wail of a baby, disturbed by the voice of a husband, righter of wrongs, or an adolescent's troubled and hyperbolic question. I now only move forward with slow steps, listening, window after window, to that accompaniment to urban solitude, so often unbearable but which, right now, I find festive. I'm moved by the steadfastness of these destinies, seemingly devoid of variety, uniformly focused on the satisfaction of their ritual needs as old as the world. I allow myself the thought that, since morning, everything that has seemed strange to me—the oppressive dialogue near the counter, the altercation between the unknown man and the young girl, then the latter's behavior, finally the atmosphere prevailing in the upper district—has only seemed so thanks to my own peculiar state of mind. Where will I be led by my distracted turn of mind if, from the start, I let myself be enticed by the slightest hints of mystery? But reality lies before my eyes in the reassuring spectacle of this humanity that smells of bad cooking and wet nappies. Every evening, in the walls of their own homes, each of them, simple, fundamentally good-hearted, asks nothing more than to reply *present!* to the call of supper.—And you, what more do you want? Come on, Fidibus, let's eat.

At the Café du Printemps, whose facade splits the darkness like a green pustule, it's only over dessert, with the last of the fellow diners gone, that I decide to raise my nose from my plate. The room is filling up with fresh arrivals, card players, drinkers who, most likely, find themselves here every evening. My presence doesn't bother them, and, like them, I can consider myself an old habitué. The plates, dishes, and lace paper that adorn the table have disappeared, to be replaced by solid glasses of dubious cleanliness filled with cheap wine by a waitress who resembles them. Light falls from two greasy bulbs.

MARCEL BÉALU

Having ordered a drink, I'm consulting, out of habit, the little notebook that serves as my aide-memoire, still unable to decipher the half-erased name and address, when an argument breaks out among a trio of card players behind me. I turn around, pretending that I have no concerns other than the wreaths of smoke wafting from the bowl of my pipe. A woman seems to be sleeping near the three men, her faded red hair spilling out over her arms folded on the table where two of the players have just abandoned their cards. One of them, looking tense and peevish, eyes ablaze, shouts: *You're cheating Squint!* The second one sneers and the black pupils of his eyes gleam with malicious curiosity as he stares at the accused man. The third party—the guilty man—has his back turned to me, but I immediately recognize him from his wretched appearance: the down-and-out from this afternoon. No doubt about it, this gentleman is pursuing me; impossible to take a step on the island without running into him! This character, whose manner and profile would be more at home among a crowd of immigrants on the deck of a steamer than in this neighborhood café, and who seemed so unimportant those few hours ago, now claims my full attention. His calmness and air of debilitation are in sharp contrast with the vociferous clamor of the other two. He has the distinctive look of someone who's been sleeping rough for a long time, but something in him, which might be called the dignity of impoverishment, raises him well above his neighbors who are blissfully unaware of their own well-dressed mediocrity. He has, this man called Squint, held onto his cards: a king, two jacks, and a queen. And my astonishing impression is that these face cards seem not unrelated to the living beings around the table, not only replicating them in image but also linked to them by other less palpable correspondences. In the very moment that this far-fetched idea strikes me, and as though to confirm it, I'm struck by a maneuver unseen by those involved in the rumpus. A finger of the bony, filthy hand holding the cards slides out the female card, flicking it to the ground where, flipping round, it falls at my feet. Then his hand, still concealed but this time so ineptly that his neighbors can't fail to see it, reverses the king positioned between the two jacks. And, as though with this final gesture the master of the game has voluntarily sacrificed the sway that he held over his two acolytes, as though he's cut the thread holding back their anger, a violent scene immediately erupts, so sordid that it's scarcely fit to be described. Suddenly on his feet, the big man yells, his jaw clenched, hands like clubs sending cards and tumblers flying. The waitress tries to intervene, but the other one, still sneering, stands up in his turn and gives her such a brutal shove that she sprawls on the floor for several minutes, underwear prominently displayed, before groaning and picking herself up. Then the brute, his eyes gleaming with cruel pleasure, as though suddenly seized with inspiration, interrupts his companion, who

MARCEL BÉALU

is hitting out while swearing, and goes one better in the language of the gutter: *What!? . . . cheating your friends? . . . And who's gonna get his sugarlumps? It's Mr. Squint, and who's gonna go woo woo? It's Mr. Squint.* His victim, still sitting, still as limp as he was under the blows, with this ruffian leaning into his face, seems to smile unconsciously and, like a well-trained dog playing along with his tormentors' game, bays in a shrill voice. *Enough already! Open your snotbox!* His persecutor, after hawking up deeply and noisily, lets fly a thick gob of spit into his mouth, which is promptly opened wide. It isn't an easy thing to depict the despicable. Frozen with shame, a sickened witness, I finally manage to get up to flee the scene. As I close the door behind me, Squint's almost expressionless face appears to be turned in my direction, while the woman, whom I thought asleep, lifts up a face that's wet with tears.

There's no better remedy for a stomach that's heaving with disgust than taking great strides to forge a path through the nighttime air. A faint sound in the wake of my footsteps soon warns me to slow down; then, anxious at being followed, I hasten toward the better-lit crossroads on the approach to the bridge. Before I've arrived there, a voice suddenly whispers, almost at the back of my neck: *Fidibus!* Stopping, I recognize Squint's pitiful features, fifty meters from mine, animated from the chase, badly shaven, and pierced by two oily lights that I can't lock onto. A remnant of professional pride—and me without a fixed profession!—would make me ashamed to be buttonholed by this individual in broad daylight, but amidst so much darkness aren't we merely two anonymous silhouettes? What's more, his voice surprises me. It possesses that particular upper-class familiarity that lower orders mistake for sympathy. *Ah, there you are*, I say. *So they didn't tear you to shreds?—No, don't go thinking they're as bad as all that ... They're still obedient even when they're angry. They're children ... Us too ...* He's panting slightly from having run, but after catching his breath he continues, astonishingly calm: *And you, Fidibus, are you obedient?* Surprised by the unexpected turn taken by the dialogue and shocked by this vagrant's presumptuousness, I reply haughtily: *How do you know my name?—I know more things in heaven and earth than are dreamed of!* he replies, so histrionically that it can only be a quip. And he promptly adds: *And if I asked how you know mine?* Not for a moment do I think of telling him the circumstances in the seedy bistro in which I heard it. Not out of pity, but because that fracas, I feel, is no concern of mine, not directly. It was, no doubt, merely the link, merely the *location* of our encounter. Something else is now involved. Perhaps I'm going to learn what it's all about. *Names mean nothing ... or very little*, he continues. But doesn't the ironical tone of his voice let it be understood that, on the contrary, names and only names

MARCEL BÉALU

are meaningful? *They can be changed like a shirt. We can get rid of one that's disagreeable. Do you want an example? The honorable individual I was talking to when you saw us this afternoon calls himself "The Professor." His name is actually Snot. Mr. Snot! You can just picture it! . . . Does he hide it because he's afraid that it'll get confused with mine,*[4] *or on account of the disgust it causes when spoken? . . . And then names wear out, get distorted, crumble away. Just as the high and mighty can always rise higher and the low can always sink lower without what's in the middle shifting, so those two words, Squint and Snot, have emerged from one and the same name. You were never in any doubt about that, were you? Nor that this professor and myself were sort of half-brothers?* While speaking he stumbles at the edge of the pavement like a beggar scrounging a handout. I make room for him, and we carry on moving forward, like two old pensioners who can no longer be driven back home by anything, anything at all, save death. We're swathed in the mist rising from the river. *People believe that names don't mean anything because ever since their far distant origins they've been reinterpreted too many times. To stick with my example, I wonder how a name has come to be distorted to this degree! A name that's so ostentatious, so resonant, ending up with us two bastards! It's really incredible, isn't it!?—But what's this name you're talking about?—Long ago, this entire island belonged to Ogyges, my respected ancestor . . .—What are you saying? Og . . . Ogyges?* Feverishly I pull out my little notebook. This time, the name that I haven't been able to read becomes clear: Og...s, that's what it is, OGYGES, Rue des Charmes. *You have to be careful*, the voice resumes after a silence. *Right from the start men maintain a wrong idea about existence that very few subsequently try to put right. Fidibus, that still doesn't mean anything, it could be a borrowed name, it doesn't seem to correspond to any reality, but as a result of calling yourself Fidibus you'll end up resembling that long, thin paper thing that anyone can set on fire. Exactly like me, Squint, descendant of the respectable and wealthy Ogyges, little by little I've acquired the appearance of this abject scrap of humanity walking along beside you, a little bent out of shape, snot-nosed and filthy ... Yes, you mustn't trust words and, even less, appearances, which are all too often determined by words. If it's an extraordinary thing that down here not one human out of two or three billion is like another, I mean hasn't arrived at the same point on the journey, some rising higher and higher, others falling lower and lower, a center shared by everyone remains constantly in existence. When will we blow up this unmoving padlock, this dead point, so that in a given moment those higher up and those lower down can join together?...*

I'm now only listening distractedly. Am I not confronted by one of those starry-eyed cranks who take the first person they come across as an opportunity to ventilate their convoluted notions at the top of their lungs? No doubt he'll shortly be telling me all about the Sephiroth and the Great Spiral. A carnival of smoke! Nevertheless, this stranger's conversation opens the door to multiple contradictions that were lying in wait to ambush me. I wonder if, with the passage of time, that which recuperates words has in fact suffered the same attrition? Or else is no longer able to avoid the consequences of a proposition such as: and if *God* had a different name? For quite a while now the blatherer has fallen silent and I continue his meditation on my own. We make our way toward the Hotel Providence and I'm about to part company with this bizarre character, now as silent as myself, when a shadow approaches at a brisk pace. I recognize the woman who was sobbing on the marble tabletop near Squint a little while ago. Under her worn and unfashionable clothes, and despite her tired and fleshy features, she isn't without a certain nobility. The sight of that creature who should have been a great beauty coming so humbly toward the down-at-heel Squint strikes me as being no less disagreeable than seeing waiters with delicate hands and patrician features serving a tableful of louts. They whisper for a moment, then the woman is lost in the darkness, but her muffled footsteps never stop following us. I daren't question my companion about what purpose he serves in life's little current. That indiscretion comes so naturally to the envious that I always bite it back when I feel it on the tip of my tongue, perhaps because I've never found it easy to reply to the question myself. Anyway, what does it matter what people *do* since, in the last analysis, all that matters is what people *are*. But, anticipating my thought, he confides to me that he's a night watchman. We've arrived at the door of my new lodgings and I mutter mechanically: *You're going to be late . . . hasn't it been dark for quite a long time already?—I'm not only required to keep an eye on its coming, but above all on its going . . .* Squint replies in the pompous tone he so readily adopts. Saying this, and just as I'm about to bid him goodbye, he extracts from his pocket an oblong card that he holds out to me, then I see the woman hurrying to catch up with my talkative friend and they both turn into a nearby alley. When they've disappeared from view I hurry over there once more before climbing the stairs of my hotel. My premonition didn't lie: the street sign reads *Rue des Charmes.* Then one of the final phrases that still sounds in my ear seems to be the echo of one heard already: *You'll certainly find what you're looking for there.* The bit of dirty yellow cardboard must have sat in his pockets for a long time. Under the name I read, in thick letters striped with two lines, OGYGES, AT THE LITTLE CURIO SHOP, *Furniture, Second-Hand Bargains, Curios, Rue des Charmes.* Yesterday I was seeking this name, searching for this street, but I've found both this evening, haven't I? I'm still very confused but I suspect that the persons who have surrounded me since this morning will help me to clear things up. A vague and unambitious

MARCEL BÉALU

hope, but one overlaid by the silhouette of the girl whom I still hope to see again and rescue (with no real idea from what). Yes, going back over my first day, her graceful face, like a pink tulip, is the one memory that I'd like to hold onto. Isn't it really her that makes me declare: I'm no longer looking for anything? So, what has this dealer in junk got to offer me? In any event, there's nothing commonplace about his guardian of darkness. While I untie my shoelaces, the printed card happens to fall at my feet, reminding me of the other card that fell near me on the floor of the bistro—the Queen, face upturned.

Stretched out on the bed, I'm about to close my eyes when a light appearing on the ceiling tells me not to fall sleep just yet. This sudden illumination comes from an apartment in the building perpendicular to mine. Has a belated traveler, someone just as hare-brained as me, also sought asylum in this hotel on the brink of going out of business? Various little noises, amplified by the silence, reveal one or more nearby presences. Soon a murmuring voice makes itself heard. I cross the room on tiptoe, only to back off at the first glimpse, although there's nothing to betray me in my little box of a room, plunged in darkness. Common sense having prevailed over surprise, I finally dare to move forward again, holding my breath. There, in the apartment with wide-open windows a few meters away, the man I've just left—him again!—is reclining in a comfortable leather armchair. No doubt he entered the apartment block shortly after me through a private entrance. His frayed trousers and sandals protrude from an elegant gray dressing gown. He's speaking quietly, his eyes directed toward a part of the room that I can't see. But for all that I strain my ears I can't make out a single word he says. When he falls silent, though each time seeming to wait for an echo, no reply reaches my ears, not even the faintest whisper. How to convey in words the frightening character of that monotonous murmur interspersed with silences in the silence of the night? I'd call out to him in order to free myself from the kind of fear that holds me in its grip, except that his increasingly strained look, its intensity evident from creased brows and raised eyebrows, persuades me that revealing my presence at that moment would not only be inconvenient, but dangerous, sacrilegious, like the cry that awakens the sleepwalker on the edge of the abyss. To what mute creature is it that Squint addresses looks as well as words? Gymnastic exertions of my body and neck only enable me to make out a little more of the imposing armchair, a brightly papered corner of the wall, and the uniformly colored carpet. I'm surprised by the quality of the lighting, the sheen of the leather, the thickness of the woolen carpet. If this is the apartment of the pitiable tramp who has just accosted me, there could be no better lesson in never trusting in appearances! The other window, further away, merely reveals the extension of the

MARCEL BÉALU

plush carpet and a little seat in the form of an X. But it occurs to me that by venturing onto the rim of the roof I'd be able see the rest of the room through that nearby opening, and so keen is my curiosity that I immediately take the risk. What then comes into view—purity of line, density of color, impeccable layout—has the effect on me of a ray of sunshine dispelling a chaos of fog, its clear opulence contrasting sharply with the wretched monochrome in which I've been drifting all day. My heart skips a beat and, delight mingling with astonishment, I need to keep a tight hold of the support so as not to let go. Outlined against the bright wall are the harmonious curves of a woman dressed in the simple lines of a scarlet gown, leaning on a kind of sarcophagus whose rectilinear silhouette accentuates her nonchalance. The attractions of her face reside less in its proportions than in a certain inner luster that radiates from every pore, adding something perfervid to her expression. Even the concentration of her gaze cannot subdue the inner flame whose light extends to her pupils. However, in addition to a kind of disorder swimming between her motionless eyelids, there's something aberrant, I don't know what, that allows a hint of the equivocal to stray over those features. Leaning forward at the risk of falling, I manage to see the top of her head. It's bald! But the form of the gleaming cranium is so harmonious that the anomaly doesn't mar her beauty. Her forehead appears to be topped by a glittering headpiece that clothes the ensemble in a beauty that exceeds strangeness—is more than human. I'm immediately convinced that this mysterious stranger is held captive there and that it's only her guardian's negligence that now allows me to catch a glimpse of her. As for Squint, I tell myself that keeping such an outstandingly attractive woman confined for his own personal gratification isn't without risk. How could she herself accept being shut up all day for the pleasure of this ugly, stunted, swarthy customer who could do with a good wash? No, I quickly banish such vulgar thoughts. Even acknowledging that it takes rare courage to knowingly assume a false self-image—far below himself—in order to keep pedants and fools at bay, the man's seductive power can only belong to a higher order, that of the spirit. A bond that is less simple and more powerful than love certainly unites him with that creature of flesh and fire, so abnormally beautiful, and who, her ambiguity notwithstanding, I'm unable to exempt from her sex. Revenge perhaps, or pity? Or who knows what complicity in such a grandiose enterprise that it needs nothing but silence and shadow for its total success.

MARCEL BÉALU

II

I climb noiselessly back over my windowsill, hasten down the stairs, slip into Rue des Charmes. Sleep is out of the question and despite the late hour my only thought is to meet Squint again. The street, or rather the retreat, terminates in a passage open to the sky with a steep descent to the river. No signs of life behind tightly closed shutters. These premises, formerly dwellings, no doubt provide warehouses for the retail business whose multiplicity of branches astonishes me. However, I notice confused activity in front of a facade with lowered blinds, ornamented by a white globe marked by big numerals. Hurrying, I rush into a kind of sloping bottle-neck, foul as a sewer, that brings this street, unattractive despite its name, out onto the quays. Above the muddy waters of the river, broad and deep at this point, the annular bridge loses itself in a foggy mirror. Returning to my point of departure I end up finding a tiny shop with a time-worn frontage just a few steps away from the Hotel Providence. I have to peer at its faded display panel for a long time to make out the words, THE LITTLE CURIO SHOP. The door surmounting the three steps embedded in the facade opens when I push it, and I edge my way into an incredible jumble of dusty objects and furniture stacked up behind. Stumbling and struggling through skeins of spider-web, I clamber over crates of second-hand utensils, piles of disintegrating books, broken crockery. Once past this bric-a-brac that no hand seems to have moved since the dawn of time, the dust becomes less thick, the stacking more methodical. A proper path now opens up, snaking between scaffolding that's still impressively high, but no longer in danger of collapsing. Has that barricade of furniture and interlocking objects been erected with the intention of deterring the eventual customer? With time and abandonment throwing up an effectual barrier, I'd never have managed to make my way through were it not for my burning desire to see Squint. Finally, I brush off the dust covering my jacket before venturing into the shadowy depths. All around me, a thousand things bear witness to every period and place on earth, from the flint tool placed on the shelf of a *Louis XV* display case to the most up-to-date surgical instrument abandoned amidst a debris of Etruscan pottery. I don't hang around to contemplate these, an entire lifetime wouldn't be enough, and I'm in a hurry to find the exit from this incredible clutter. Several times, someone surging from the most unsuspected corners gives me a bad start; it's only fragments of a broken mirror

MARCEL BÉALU

reflecting my own image back at me. At other times I break out in a sudden sweat, stopping to ask myself what I've come looking for in these mausoleums. A part-open door under which a little bit of light is filtering leads me, after having stumbled against three steps, to a new room, bigger than the previous ones and similarly filled to the brim. But everything here is tidy, signaling the recent activity of brooms and feather dusters. One can move about easily, and I quickly arrive before a third door also surmounting three steps. This opens onto a huge metal-framed hangar, a much bigger shop than the two previous ones. And I haven't come to the end of the surprises in store for me. Just as every reply annuls its question only to give rise to one or many more, replying to which will in turn engender a multitude of questions, so seven or eight depots open before my steps, no less crammed full, and each one permitting access by means of various tributaries to still others. Some are sheltered by glass roofs, others covered with simple tarpaulins or open to the skies. In these latter, the heterogeneous piles are rusting or perishing under awnings that do little to protect them from the elements. The abandonment of these locations surprises me less than the quantity, the variety and, above all, the indubitable value of the objects everywhere accumulated. I can't believe that a mere dealer in used goods is in possession of such wares. In this universe of forsaken items, a true global flea market, how can buyers recognize, locate what they want? Most of those who come in here must go away again empty-handed. There's too much of everything to pause in front of any one thing.

Just now, in a fever to discover the trail of the night watchman and the mysterious bald woman, I inspected every room, poked about everywhere. But, tired of the disorder, I'm now only anxious to get out. By sheer luck, for I could have wandered in this labyrinth forever, some further steps bring me to a spacious shop with large display windows that I immediately recognize. The dummy crudely assembled by the girl is still there; once more I see the coat, the hat, the gloves. As I've been able to confirm from the outside, every item of furniture, restored, varnished, offers itself to the gaze in gleaming good order, no doubt polished daily. In no hurry to get out now that I know the street is just a few steps away, I decide to do what I certainly should have done right from the start: shout out. *Is anyone there?* . . . and in a louder and higher pitched voice, *Hello! Anyone?* I'm so convinced of being alone that I don't bother waiting for a reply. But, nearby, the clear voice of a young person puts a stop to my yells. *Not so much noise, sir!* It's the dummy, or rather the young girl whom I mistook for the dummy. Seated there, hat on head, she mumbles a little on removing it. *I didn't expect you so soon* . . . What does time matter to me who's been trying for eons to find my way through this omnium-gatherum! Who cares what time it is in these places piled high with the Earth's accumulated history? While she flutters in confusion, I look at her more closely, brazenly noting her features, enjoying her blushes and her growing discomfort. Cruelly I even insist on staring more and more intently into her eyes. *But do by all means take off your coat too. Carry right on as if I weren't here.* The irony of this allusion goes beyond what I intended. The young girl's face colors and her eyes moisten with humiliation, as though before a misunderstanding that can't possibly be put right. They continue nevertheless to look courageously at me, and, somewhat ashamed, it's me who retreats to my own concerns. *So, where is your night watchman? ... Yes, Squint, your night watchman. Surely such big shops can't be left without a night watchman?* Here I am, now saying his name almost proudly, the very individual whom I regarded with a pity that borders on repugnance, as though to demonstrate to this child that I'm not just any casual passerby. *Oh, there are so many abandoned things, you know,* she replies at last, nervously; ... *untold riches. No one will take them, though, nobody seems to see them.* (No need to squeeze in order to hold her frail arms, almost completely encircled by my fingers.) *Do these abandoned things really need a night watchman while the whole world is sleeping? Wouldn't they prefer total silence to the noise of shoes tramping all round them, since there won't be any burglars breaking in at night ...* The rise and fall of the young woman's pullover reveals the emotion with which these rapid words are uttered. A name is traced with sky-blue thread on this pretty, pale beige pullover: *Corinne*. Isn't it charming? And this name rises toward me, or falls, like the heart hidden underneath, in the depths of her blood. But abruptly, shaking free of my grip: *Let me go!* She must have noticed my distraction. In fact, I've started to think again about the apparition for which I'm here. *But isn't there someone I can see . . .* I say at last to save face.

You're right, she murmurs, *I'm nobody, not worth as much as the items that interest you so much, those ones there that you're looking at . . .* And coldly, with renewed awareness of the situation: *What is it you want? If it's a matter of the night watchman, he isn't available right now. Otherwise, do you think you'd have been able to see everything and inspect the most out-of-the-way rooms . . .* In saying these words her anxious curiosity seeks to find from my look or my response what exactly it is that I've discovered. But I remain impassive, and she continues: *You're in a privileged position, monsieur. My job was to keep you here among these appealing up-to-date items, to make you admire the good taste of our artistic and domestic displays, the range and proven comfort of our model layouts, the variety of our decors of all types . . . But I got here too late. I expected you at the main door and not at this concealed entrance which anyway I thought was bolted . . . I'm not*

MARCEL BÉALU

very sure . . . I'm never very sure of anything . . . Her words now betray an infinite weariness. Abrupt changes of tone indicate the sudden gaps in her train of thought. *Ah, I'm left too much on my own. It's so long since we've seen a customer, a visitor! Your arrival has left me completely at a loss. God knows everything I dream up to keep a little bit of order in this chaos! Only very old employees were here before me, old men and women, and old people turn everything upside down before they die, as though they get a nasty pleasure from that . . . How can I be in two places at once, the cellar and the attic, the cart and the mill, keeping watch on Rue des Charmes and drying my tears in here, all at the same time? . . . I can't carry on like this! Whatever I do, wherever I go, this never-ending task that's beyond my strength shuts me off from real life. However much I try to sort out what can still pass for new in all this lumber, however much I polish, arrange things, stick things back together as I'm supposed to, it's all a waste of time . . . I'm really left too much on my own.* No doubt sensing my pity, she starts over again: *It's better this way, sooner or later I'd have been obliged to own up to what you've found out: this property's state of neglect, the poor condition of the goods, the complete lack of management, of accountancy, of maintenance, in a word the imminent ruin of these commercial premises that used to be so prosperous and that supplied the whole world. How could it be any different? The fate of an enterprise of this magnitude can't be left in hands as flimsy as mine . . . A whole army of shop assistants is needed to put everything in order, not a night watchman.* She turns her back to me, is about to disappear. But I've seen the tears start from her eyelids. *Corinne!* The child who's forgiven isn't as quick to throw itself into its mother's arms as Corinne is to turn back to me. *I haven't taken advantage of that freedom that you're blaming me for, not at all, I haven't seen anything, I ran through all the depots, and from the order and cleanliness here where you are I'd never have suspected what you've been telling me. Believe me, I'm still amazed. I've got thousands of questions . . .* The sincerity of these words reassures her and now there's an almost joyful look in her eyes. But she interrupts me. *Not here! We can't speak here.* And before I have time to admit to her why I've come here (perhaps because I now have some scruples to confess to her), she pulls me out of the shop. On each side of the avenue, trees pruned of their branches look like gibbets on top of which gigantic spiders nailed upside down dangle their legs in the twilight. We quickly cross the bridge at the end of which a road stretches out under the leaves, a true green corridor. Why so much mystery? Corinne smiles and it's the first time I've seen her smile. But almost immediately her face resumes its somber expression.

As soon as I saw you, I thought of warning you, Monsieur? . . .—Fidibus.—That's right, Fidibus. I was told that a certain Fidibus would show up for the job of representative.

MARCEL BÉALU

You'll get him to sign the usual papers . . . I'm about to interrupt, to say that there's a misunderstanding, that I'm no longer a representative, that I don't want to become one, that all that's nothing but a bad joke, that in any event I'd never let myself get trapped in such a fateful business, one so little suited to my abilities. But, gathering these thoughts from my look, the young woman continues: *When you came in, you didn't talk about that job, but asked to see the night watchman. So, I got flustered. All the more because when I saw you, I was no longer set on getting you to sign the paper in question. I realized that you were completely innocent . . .* Eyes lowered, she hesitates. I feel her disclosures slipping away from me. She's waiting for a word of encouragement and idiot that I am, I show her nothing but impatience. Taking hold of her hands, I look at her gently. Her eyes suddenly go moist when I caress her brow and she murmurs these strange words: *Oh yes, it was high time you came back!* No doubt she wants to seal this old childhood pact in whose tenderness she still believes? I squeeze her in my arms, cover her eyes with kisses. *You don't seem in any doubt at all about where we are . . .* , she begins with just a touch of anger in her voice (and her little foot stamps the ground in a movement that makes me smile). So saying, she parts the tall reeds that separate us from the river and the island appears before us, a somber mass pinpricked by winking lights, a gigantic vessel borne on clouds. *No matter what you think, this neighborhood isn't a place for idylls, not at all! Monsieur Fidibus arrives and pretends to take his ease just like that, to amuse himself without being answerable to anyone, an affluent stranger going incognito. But there are thousands who would also like such independence. Me too, you know, I'm sick of being the custodian of a dead world, I don't care how big it is! I'd really like to abandon it, although my tiredness isn't the same as yours. But WE no longer have the right! Nor even the power!* She adds feebly; *I sometimes get the impression that I'm being kept under observation too, by those things I'm supposed to watch over.* In other times, other places, I would have been annoyed by such protestations. Every woman knows to perfection this role of teacher, no doubt assigned to her by nature. But here and now, in spite of her slightly playful tone of voice, a real anxiety is revealed by the deep seriousness that her sad and gleaming eyes don't seek to disguise. At this moment, two surprising words emerge like a breath from her mouth, so that I'm not sure of having heard them: *My love . . .* Perhaps these two words are nothing but a binding spell, a means of binding me to her words. For a long time, she remains thoughtful, then, changing the topic, confides that she never knew her father. Her mother married again, and she lives near her stepfather and mother. *I'm often alone in the house with that man. I'm afraid of him. Everybody on the island calls me "the professor's daughter."* (I see once more the brutal face of the man near the counter, watching for Corinne passing by.) *It's him, not my father. He's called "professor" because he knows everything, because he's learned everything, but his knowledge is nothing but dead knowledge. The fact is that he deals in used goods and in antiques of the spirit, just like all the others, his philosophy is nothing but a coat of varnish on old furniture, old bronzes, old bonzes. He's ignorant of everything that's alive, every moment of the present, everything whose chance arrival interferes with his notions ... For example, he doesn't know* (a long laugh gurgles in her throat like the cooing of two doves suddenly awoken), *he doesn't know that we're here this evening, you and me, and that we're going to have a baby.*

What a mockery! Through my fault a supplementary creature will be added to the miserable common lot, will sprout, develop, pointlessly suckle its milk, pointlessly grow stronger, maybe also become, in adulthood, a representative like me—without representing anything. The revelation evokes a multitude of memories. This island on which I thought I'd never before set foot: haven't I in fact come back to reconnoiter a very old adventure, the start of which was marked by the half-obliterated little phrase in my notebook? Was it Corinne or her clothed double that I perceived back then, behind the display? I now clearly remember the rendezvous at the tip of the island where the stream of water, in dividing, slowly erodes the extremity of the bank's shelf, stripping its roots bare and revealing, under the scree of the arable ground, the superimposed and stratified layers of subsoil. We'd scrambled down that short slope in order to see, some fifty meters distant, in the middle of the water, a big cluster of silvered foliage obscured by the pulsating surface. *We've got to go there . . .* Corinne had said, pointing toward that little island of willows. And I now understood that the young woman, counting her weapons and preparing them for combat, had planned, considered this rendezvous down to its smallest detail, decided on it. No doubt long before knowing me she had foreseen and weighed up the perils and pleasures without knowing who would share them. Thus, there stood before me, freed from coquettish finery, a superb, smooth white beast, the stupendous, impure animal created to remind the prideful spirit of its folly. A scattering of droplets splashed over me, depriving me of that vision. I stripped off, hid my clothes near hers and quickly joined her. My movements in the liquid element rediscovered a lost rhythm, a forgotten solemnity. I felt my strength match the agility of that disheveled fawn, glimpsed for an instant in the light and who now swam some lengths ahead. The current didn't seem violent although it pulled us back at the slightest relaxation of effort; so we made only slow progress, striking through heavy water whose depths bore us up, but we had to continually conquer it so as not to be conquered. Assailed over the centuries by that enormous liquid mass, how was it that the island hadn't been swept away? For the islet that we reached to remain unshaken above such gulfs its crown of sand and foliage must surely conceal a spur of rock. She laughed, she sang, and we ran like lunatics in the narrow cove isolated from the rest of the world. Birdsong and the murmuring of the willows surrounded us. Corinne's lips had the warm, slightly acid taste of fallen cherries baked in the grass by the sun. And her legs opened under me on the fine sand as I knew that terrifying wonderment of forever separating a unique and marvelous fruit from the tree that had nurtured it to maturity. Luminous ambush! Resurgence of a distant memory, but my complete surrender to which was forbidden by the haunting spell of Squint's mysterious guest. Without surprised delight and without fear I learn that I'm about to become a father, I feel the birth of my son as the advent of a catastrophe. As regards my going away, my business, my real identity, everything, everything, Corinne knows nothing, has learned nothing. For her I'm still the chance arrival of the first day. Doesn't this sweet face, pink as a tulip, hide just as heavy a load of secrets from me? No, hers were of another kind: secrets of the blood, to which she's just admitted.

Corinne has disappeared, and with determined steps I reascend the narrow neck of Rue des Charmes, single-mindedly obsessed by Squint's beautiful visitor or captive. I must at all costs see her again. But, since I only owe my discovery of their interview to an exceptional relaxation of hitherto inviolate laws, I'm afraid that if my curiosity is revealed to him, he'll then arrange things so as to frustrate it. My vanity takes pride in having learned as by right of the double life led by that ragged wretch, a laughingstock for some, figure of contempt for all. My basic smugness is crowned by the thought that, cunning though he is, the rascal doesn't play the game of impoverishment as well as I play the game of wealth (in taking up leisurely residence in this downtrodden district). The door that I noticed a short while ago under the white globe, hanging like a cut-price moon with its sales ticket stuck on above, outlines a thin rectangle of light. I enter. Instead of the low room, worn benches, the naked girls, the fixed-price orgy into which I thought I'd tumble, I find myself in the thick of a dense crowd in a long, smoke-filled room. At the far end, a speaker on a platform is gesticulating. I'm prevented from moving by my position between the door and the back of those who were last to arrive. However, I'd really like to hear the distant speech that seems to concern salesmen, managers, representatives. Shouts erupt at each of those titles, met by almost imploring responses of *Shh! Shh!* Fists are raised, a tumult gathers, incited down there by the voice that I can't quite manage to hear. Let's hope that no one turns round! I imagine that the role of "representative" is written all over my face. Singled out, how would I declare my innocence? The presence of the professor, whom I

MARCEL BÉALU

finally manage to see on the platform, only partly reassures me. The man doesn't know me, and he's so far off! I'd be lynched a score of times before he showed up. And would he come to my defense, or would he merely hear my cries for help? Wouldn't he sooner incite the crowd against me? I'm very much intrigued by the impression of expectancy that hovers in the room despite the disorder and the clamor. Evidently this speech is nothing more than a prelude, the sanctified blather prefacing the unity of soul requisite to the fulfillment of the mystery. The speaker now flails frantically, something all the more bewildering in that no one is contradicting him. Aren't all these people only angry with themselves, aren't they only seeking an end to their boredom? Where are the administrators hiding, the managers, members of the Administrative Committee, why do none of them come running either to lend support to these outcries or else demonstrate their utter fatuousness? All the denizens of the island are there, the entire tightly packed herd that clogged my steps a few moments ago, the stumbling herd with hostile faces. Yes. They're all there. All except one. Except the one I'm seeking. The night watchman! No doubt he's alone and roaming the empty streets. While the populace shuts itself in this smoke-filled room, he, the outcast, is going about his task. On the platform the professor succeeds the orator who spoke first. I learn the secret of his power from what I hear of his speech; he doesn't bring any words to the crowd; he is its word.

Suddenly, in the middle of a turbulent group, I see Squint's sorry partners from the card game in the Café du Printemps. One of the two is exultant, face afire, and the other's jet-black eyes sparkle like an animal about to receive its daily feed. At that moment it becomes impossible to make out anything whatsoever in the cacophony of cursing, laughing, or harsh reproaches. What spectacle have they all been promised?

A veritable outburst of howls greets a new arrival on the stage that has just been vacated by the professor and the various speakers. I myself am no longer listening, no longer able to tear my eyes away from the platform where I've just recognized my unknown woman, Squint's prisoner! She stands in her dark red gown, its harmonious curves outlined against the bright wall, a specter offered up to all, a great archangel suspended above this human storm as though to subdue it, calm it, and, it seems to me, to become its prey. Trying to push my way toward her I'm once more stuck fast in the shifting swamp like a knife blade in flesh. And suddenly, by dint of staring at the distant face beyond that compact mass of people, although I'm prevented from seeing it clearly by the radiance of the massive forehead absorbing it into a halo, it seems to me that it moves not one iota, and that, regardless of distance, the axis of her gaze remains rigidly fixed on this minuscule point that, among so many others, must be mine. Perhaps everyone receives an identical impression, imagining that the woman with the glittering helmet is there for him, for him alone, and that to him alone she silently dictates her orders. But little by little, the fixity of her gaze reminds me of something other than the immobility of a painted image. Where have I already seen this living gaze *resting on me*? At that thought I force my gaze elsewhere, fearful of becoming the plaything of some phantom. All around me faces look continually agitated, mouths twisting although no sounds emerge, and all that animation submerged in the most absolute silence is something so monstrous that I'm seized by a desire to flee. I hastily retrace my steps back along the length of the room toward the exit as though driven by the violence of despair. If only it had formed in my brain alone, the supernatural vision. I'm revolted by the thought that this multitude has the same idol as me, that my most secret obsession has become food for all. And while they launch themselves toward her, arms flailing, I flee on account of the same fierce decency that, until now, has kept me at a distance from her presence. I've no sooner taken a few steps in the dark street than I almost bump into the redheaded woman whom I saw behind the night watchman's rags. I thought I'd seen her just now in the front row of the assistants. Has she, with her almost deceptive way of letting herself be pulled by invisible strings, made her way back across the room in my wake? *I'm Corinne's mother*, she says, staring me straight in the eye. And while I bow to her, she adds: *You can call me Beatrice.* Her gaze tells me that she knows all about my relations with her daughter and my embarrassment correspondingly increases. She immediately continues, *Monsieur Fidibus, you love Corinne, don't you . . . ?* (any thought of reply is precluded by the tone of these words). *Very well! Go away with her, leave this island. Neither of you are involved with what's going on here.*

Despite her urgency, why does it seem that, more than me, it's herself that she wants to persuade? I try to reply firmly, but I'm scarcely more certain of what I myself have to say. *Buying, selling,* she murmurs, *buying selling . . . today that's just a false front concealing a subtler activity. Ah, this activity that I don't know about, I'd like not to know that I'm ignorant of it, just like the others. It used to be that the job of representative was straightforward. My gentlemen canvassed the island in order to sell our furniture, second-hand goods, curios. Life was meaningful. They collected plenty of orders and I was happy to expedite them. That work had a purpose. An Office for Restocking took it upon itself to repurchase at low prices furniture that was damaged, worn out, or that some people had been forced to resell out of necessity. Business was flourishing. But little by little the sellers came to outnumber the buyers, soon there were no more buyers. Already the representatives' only purpose was to act as buffers in the event of a disturbance. Do you see? . . . Everyone's goods piled up in storage while the inhabitants lived miserably in empty apartments. It was then that the professor proposed his solution: to completely reorganize the enterprise by transforming the inhabitants' dwellings into new warehouses. It seems that that's what's happened, but it only seems so, because even though the laziness or indifference of the island's bosses has allowed the professor to do whatever he wants, those bosses still exist, no less so for being anonymous, even invisible.—And what do the residents of the district live on?—They draw a salary, monsieur. That's what I think is harmful, for these wages give them the illusion of freedom. For a long time now, everyone has been aware of the uselessness of their work (since there aren't any customers). Luxury isn't enough to give them the feeling of being "at home" that they've lost. It's as though they've sensed that they'll never again be comfortably at home . . . Coming and going again at the requisite times without knowing where they're coming from or where they're going to, they're remunerated for this daily coming and going, for which they have no use. What's to be done? This sense of emptiness leaves lots of them with a bad conscience that drives them to wholesale ransacking. They have a blind confidence in the professor, who's careful to maintain this sentiment. His latest notion is to sell off the business, to dispose of the whole island. But who'll be prepared to take on such a purchase? A few people who vaguely understand that this state of stagnation will lead to a collapse can only hope for a resumption of business activities. Don't confine canvassing to the limits of the island, they declare, let it be extended to the city of A . . . , then to the whole world. They know that, given time, the outcome will be the same, but while waiting it would at least be possible to live a comfortably normal life, the life they had before. Those who prefer this . . . innocent solution (and also, in my opinion, no less mistaken than the first solution) are fewer and fewer because the Management to whom representations should be made has become completely invisible. That's the worst of it, you see, and far from the strangest. Shareholders, Directors, Managers, Department supervisors, the executive chairman himself, they've all vanished as though swallowed up by the ground. The night watchman is the only one left.*

And yet our firm has a name: Ogyges. That predecessor started out very modestly, no doubt as an itinerant trader in used goods. Already his first shop, the "Little Curio Shop" on Rue des Charmes, carried no more than an obscure company name. Then the business expanded to the point where the whole district became these big department stores that you've been able to see, and that have finally become pointless. Corinne has been made responsible for nothing but the persistence of a memory. Today no one still remembers Monsieur Ogyges apart from his direct descendants, the night watchman and the professor. They themselves only remember him in order to argue about the upkeep of the

MARCEL BÉALU

premises that he founded, about which they have very different ideas, the one no less than the other. We've arrived at the approach to the bridge. Beatrice continues: *Don't thank me for these declarations by telling me that you love Corinne . . . There's something that attracts you through her, but it's not her that you love. Meanwhile, through you, it's you that she loves, not the representative that you'd like to be but the stranger that you are.*—No doubt you're right about that, but Corinne still believes in her task, and by joining this community, I'd maybe manage to restore order to it . . .—It's important that Corinne has faith in you, but she's the one whose trust will be lost through contact with you. There can be no way forward here other than marching alongside the professor, torch in hand. Afterward we can start over again, no longer buying and selling but* making, *constructing furniture and necessities, one at a time. Do you see? Nothing will give us back the appetite for work until we've destroyed everything. But as for you, save yourself before you lose this appetite, flee from that thing which is our only remedy, save Corinne!* This plea, welling from the shadows, speaks in the voice of good sense. But now I refuse to remove myself from the island, because the island shelters the *other.* How admit that to this woman who is Corinne's flesh and blood? And when everyone goes back to working with their hands, the produce of this labor will rapidly exceed needs once more. Business transactions, trading, buying, selling will once again be unavoidable. It's the height of naïveté to think that *making* is all that's needed. Time unmakes, makes, remakes, not endlessly, but until an inevitable explosion occurs. Everything returns, terminates in this point of utter destitution. *For God's sake,* I cry, *I grant you that the remuneration you're allowed by those against whom you're rebelling is meager and the life it allows is scant at best, but it's enough for you to live on. Safeguard your earnings and leave the false wealth of these goods to the dunghill that'll follow on faster than any rebellion. As far as I'm concerned, that's what I've decided and I'm sure that Corinne will soon share my opinion . . .* My words go somewhat beyond my intentions, something that often happens when I try to convince. Confronted with Beatrice's downcast face I fall abruptly silent. It's then that she murmurs with an absent air: *There isn't a salary that doesn't cost something . . . May we learn what we can still live for before it's too late.* And while she looks at me, I suddenly recognize the very same look that transfixed mine at a distance of thirty feet from the height of the platform. *I can see that my warnings are wasted. It isn't Corinne who has the main claim on you, it's the other, "she who has no purpose in life" . . . Corinne is a new barrier that you've yet to overcome. Like me, you don't know how to choose. A solitary stranger, you were able do anything whatever, nothing tied you to these objects from the past that we curse without having the courage to do without. Corinne will teach you to love them, for you, the mystery will be no more than a symbol, a stuffed Liberty for electoral meetings, a Goddess of straw for the*

　　　　　　　　　　　　　　MARCEL BÉALU

altar of the church of tourists. So, don't you know that She, too, that other whose distance you find so provoking, is ALIVE? Beatrice's reproach moves me, though I feel it penetrate like a monstrous jealousy. Doesn't she love with the same insatiable love both Corinne and the remarkable woman whose image pursues me? But I don't want to protest, sensing that her confession's most desperate moment is at hand. It didn't fall from her lips, but I was able to read it clearly on her features, which crimsoned with that flush which, even when we are alone, afflicts us on remembering very old words or acts. *You know that the professor isn't Corinne's father . . .* she whispered; *but you don't know who her father is?—The night watchman?* I cried. At these words, Beatrice once more becomes the woman that I saw in the Café du Printemps, her eyelids at last hiding the gaze that no longer seems to belong to her, sobbing between her folded arms, under the frozen fire of her long hair.

These explanations, like the somewhat confused ones of Squint and Corinne, provide me with a different version of the same enigma without supplying the key. They illuminate things from another angle without revealing the underside—which is all that matters. But I'm beginning to get the impression that perhaps the truth only wears the mask of mystery so as not to admit defeat, surrounded on all sides, like the cornered beast who, under the upraised knife, sends out such a pathetic look that the armed hand needs more willpower to merely lower itself than that required by all the trappings of the hunt. My interlocutor walks away, and I follow her. After having threaded her way through a maze of little lanes behind the Hotel Providence she heads toward a tall, square building amidst the scrubby vegetation that reaches as far as the tip of the island. Of the leafy shade that formerly surrounded it there still remains the tufted skeleton of an absurd tamarisk, like a gigantic insect clutching onto a doghouse, and old leafless spindle trees inscribing their complicated hieroglyphs on each side of the approach road. When Beatrice has disappeared through a concealed entrance, I go up to the facade that a facetious owner has embellished with an imposing door of faux bronze with fluted columns, and I can't repress an instinctive shudder of aversion in recognizing in the embrasure the man whom everywhere I hear named as "the professor." *Well, well! Monsieur Fidibus! . . . What a pleasant surprise!* he exclaims in a voice that strives for geniality but is full of self-conceit. And I'm invited into a narrow office smelling of fumigation. *So? Still strolling around? . . .* I divine a thousand avid papillae under the cold and meek mask. Souls condemned to sterility believe in the necessity of interposing an impassive veil between themselves and the world, thinking that they're concealing their cruel egotism, but little by little the features of greed show through, sometimes exploding at the end of their lives into those ferocious grimaces that populate padded cells. My interlocutor's envelope of ice, though still solidly attached, is no more convincing than his unobservant way of looking at you. I hear sounds of rummaging in the neighboring room and hope that Beatrice or Corinne entering unexpectedly at any moment will release me from an awkward situation. But the headmaster of the place will have forbidden women from entering his bureau. Seeing his advantage (I'm pretty intimidated), he carries on interrogating me as though I'm his latest pupil. *What do you do for a living, Monsieur Fidibus? . . . You seem to come from nowhere and we run into you everywhere. It would be amusing to play the part of outsider if this island still had room for spectators or bit part players. Alas, everyone must be an actor and know their role!—Know their role, that's it exactly* . . . I sputter, for the sharp voice of the person facing me is impressive; *and, you see, I don't, any more than the majority of my neighbors seem to . . .—You're mistaken*, he interrupts, making it clear that any resistance would be detrimental to my education. And, with flattery in his voice: *However, you seem intelligent . . . There's nothing to prevent you from joining our ranks, from you too knowing your role . . . We're on this Earth, we're even on a tiny point of the Earth, where human problems have crystallized to such an extent, contracted to such an extent, that short of deliberately assuming the mantle of madness, it's impossible not to see them . . . You've certainly found out that, previously, this*

island was burdened by a precarious retail business: the
Galeries Ogyges. An army of employees wasted their lives . . .

The more he talks, the more I'm astonished to hear, in
slightly different language, the same exposé, the same
invites or reproaches that I heard from Corinne and
Beatrice. Really! So, it's possible, starting from the same
evidence, to arrive at diametrically opposite conclusions!
Never have I been so clearly confronted with the irrel-
evance of all opinions. *Today, the privileges of the upper*
echelons remain, but they're in ruins, like these multiple
warehouses that each day deteriorate a little more. But the
siren that transforms the island's inhabitants into servile
menials continues to sound at the set time. Because each
day they forget a little more that choices must be made,
these slaves have become an amorphous mass, a kind of gas
that's beneficial or harmful depending on how the wind
blows. It's up to us, I mean to say to certain people, maybe
to one person only (a light of triumph gleams in his eyes)
to take on the responsibility of deciding whether to be brake
or accelerator on that slope that runs ever more steeply from
yesterday to tomorrow, to be the clear-sighted intermedi-
ary of the future or the RE-PRE-SEN-TATIVE *of the past.*
All this in the flat, disabused voice of someone always
mindful of his superiority. I'm also startled when the
pedant throws the penultimate noun in my face like an
insult, forcefully articulating each syllable. Could it be

that I, who don't want to have a past, look in this man's eyes like the representative of the past? Can it be that a moment's joke has resulted in such a misunderstanding? I had to correct it at once so that it didn't give rise to another, itself the source of infinite others. *Wait, wait!* And without pausing for breath, I own up to my true identity, recount my return to the island, state my intention of remaining (without, of course, mentioning my real motives). The better to convince him, I turn on the tears, sniffle maybe a little too loudly. And it's his turn to be startled, so abruptly that I remember his name: *Snot.* My God! Just as, moments earlier, the title of representative cut me to the quick, this sniffle, which he takes as a vulgar allusion to his name, has stung his pride. What vanity under our self-importance. *You know as well as I do*, he continues in a more conciliatory tone, probably thinking it useful to apologize for a reproach that I've been deft enough (?) to throw back in his face; *you know as well as I do that representatives no longer represent anything at all, eh?* (he gives me a friendly nudge) . . . *no longer represent anything other than those idiotic surnames that we inherited from our forebears, stupidly deformed over time, eh?* (another nudge) . . . . *And even if you were a representative of the past, you'd become a representative of the future, that's all.* He's still condescending, but toward a subordinate whose high qualities and future promise can no longer be overlooked. I shake hands, not without distaste. His belated friendliness is surely based on an error; I've shown myself to be naive and sincere, for him signs of mediocrity, and he thought me sarcastic and overbearing, defects that he appreciates as marks of superiority. We're about to go our separate ways when Beatrice appears on the doorstep of the neighboring apartment. Seeing me, she quickly puts a finger to her mouth, but this gesture of silence transforms itself so quickly into an innocuous wiping of her upper lip that I don't know whether it's meant for me or her now silent husband. Given that uncertainty, I think it's best for now to remain tight-lipped about my matrimonial intentions. My future father-in-law seems so firmly convinced that the sole purpose of my visit is to gain his advice ... No point in disabusing him!—*Beatrice, my wife* ... he says. My decision to say nothing about the young woman is bolstered by the fact that she hasn't revealed our relationship, or the one I have with Corinne. In short, this professor, knowing everything, doesn't know much.

The strange signifier of silence continues to puzzle me. Are they both against me? I can't believe they're against the young woman. Eager to make sense of this new mystery, I'm ready to withdraw when I'm disconcerted by a portrait I see in the neighboring room, through a door that remains wide open. It's the bald woman, no doubt about it! Everything that was troubling me melts away and I walk like an automaton toward that figure. She's

MARCEL BÉALU

painted in rudimentary strokes that suggest a rapid sketch, but faced with the extraordinary resemblance, how regain my self-possession? I'm returned to reality by the voice of the professor, who, thankfully behind me, doesn't see how dumbstruck I am. From his explanations I can assume that he takes my sudden attention for artistic curiosity. Mockingly, with an affected banter that typifies the man: *Is that what you like, bald as baby's bottom?—How odd* . . . And I can't stop myself from adding, *Who is it?—Ha ha!* he responds, suddenly vulgar; *that's got you interested, eh? It looks,* he cries to his wife, *like he's keen on Lolotte. I'm sorry, my friend, just like me, you'll have to make do with that picture* . . . And he explains to me, in all seriousness, that this portrait, which he ranks with the most magnificent works of modern art (no doubt on account of the strangeness of the gaze and the bizarre absence of hair), was executed among the aboriginal natives of the Chinese mountains on the borders of North Assam and Burma. The painting is the faithful reproduction of an idol of the Lolos tribe who, centuries ago, withdrew into the mountains in order to escape conquest by the Chinese. According to the painter, a European adventurer, the Lolos lead a primitive life in huts of beaten earth, under the leadership of hereditary chieftains. Holders of secrets that enable the transmutation of personality, their Goddess isn't a myth but a kind of sacred personage resulting from an amalgam of moral and physical qualities taken from the finest specimens of the clan. They adore her under the name of MUTA. *As you might expect*, the professor adds, *that's all utter nonsense! The artist in question, a prisoner of these tribes for many long years, must have gone native and smoked opium. I myself think that this portrait that I call Lolotte is purely imaginary, the product of his visions . . .* The denial of the irrational, while it facilitates our relations with our fellow men, in no way dispels the inscrutable mysteries surrounding us. These comments allow me to recover my composure. Before turning away, I throw a last glance into the office in order to see Beatrice. Sitting down, she seems to be asleep, her head bowed into her folded arms on the table. Now I can put a name to the woman I want to see again: Muta. But who is she? Evidently the professor was making fun of me with his tale of adventurer artist-painter and Tibetan prisoner. I haven't gone fifty meters from the house before that thought makes me turn back. Corinne's father-in-law comes to meet me as though having suspected my return. *Oh no, oh no . . .* he replies to my concerns. *In order to calm the emotions of our audience, which are dangerously high-pitched, we've been obliged to prescribe a tranquilizer. I had a kind of mannequin put together in the image of that effigy to act as a soporific for the crowd. It's that replica of Lolotte that you saw my boy . . . A deception if you like, a mystification . . . certainly not a mystery.* Is he still pulling my leg? I hurry back to the Hotel Providence, climb up floor by floor. Immediately, it seems to me that I haven't left my room, that everything that's happened to me since I went in search of Squint has flashed by in a few seconds. The two windows situated a little further down are still wide open and lit up. I lean out, trembling all over, and once more see the night watchman sunk in the big armchair. But for all that I climb out onto roof ledge, I'm no longer able to see his mysterious prisoner. But she's there, I'm sure of it, recording the words that Squint dictates to her. My intuition doesn't deceive me. While I lean forward in a useless effort, holding my breath, a step lighter than a sigh approaches, I hear the imperceptible swish of a gown round a body in motion, and suddenly the big woman with the mad features appears in her entirety in my field of view, clothed this time in the qualities of a real presence. Her eyes, from which all the stars flash out, send the combined beams of the nocturnal firmament back toward my shadow. Vision of a moment! In that moment the gutter gives under my weight and with a frightful crash I tumble down fifteen meters into the courtyard.

III

Dying in a dream often coincides with awakening. I'm not dead. Padded with tarred sackcloth, the awning that overhangs the corridor door has generously cushioned my fall. But through a curious effect of doubling, the shock seems to have delivered me to another, more profound life. Is it me under the single ray of moonlight reaching the courtyard flagstones, gasping and moaning like a mangled white victim amid shards of glass and splintered lath? Heart of lead, lunar heart, keep a hold of this body made of too heavily rolled-up paper! While shadows will busy themselves around it, I'll take flight, a pure spirit freed from all ties. Across the island, decor of my delirium, the quick glance allowed me here and there by the respite from my passage will be like the magnesium flash that steals the snapshot of a grimace from the harmonious progression of images. Walls overturn, invisible drawbridges lay themselves down, and every roof is lifted before this phantasmal Fidibus, whiter than his mortal remains wrapped in a shroud of moonlight.

Head in the clouds, lightheaded, see how I soar! Heavy doors crumble where, timid witness, puny hero, I'd hardly dared to knock before now without trembling. Who lives in that room? Rather ask, who is dying? On a rotten pallet, ragged brats ceaselessly repeat, *I'm hungry*. Nearby, a drunk woman stares at them, stupefied. Is there nothing left to sell, Mr. Dilettante? Let's go into the neighboring room, let's sneak in among these perfumed spectators. Fashion show. *"Five minutes to midnight." Very stylish two-piece negligee . . .* murmurs the MC while a pretty woman jots down *five hundred thousand francs* with a pretty flourish of her pencil. What's the use of so many shouts, so many hate-filled words? I have no voice; my mouth opens and shuts pathetically. In whose name would I speak, in the name of what? An outsider, I can only be the representative of another world. My virtuous indignation as incognito witness is worthless. Go away, onlooker, or learn your role better! A pure spirit stays deaf, a pure spirit stays mute. The river cloaks everything in a carapace of mist, excellent for cushioning shocks. Armored by this cotton wool, I'm no longer Fidibus, no longer a representative. Head in the clouds, lightheaded, see how I fly! What I have to say is elsewhere. Penetrating to the depths of my heart, the moon knows it.

Where are we? The shopfront reads *The Little Curio Shop*. A drab and luminous eye hangs from the ceiling, brief

MARCEL BÉALU

brightness from time to time on the nape of the neck. *Stop, go! Stop, go!* The naked crowd scurries at the barked command of an invisible loudspeaker, an anonymous herd in which no face is recognizable. Take your place in its ranks Mr. Moribund, ready to surrender your miserable quarter of an hour at any price. The human tide fills the galleries in a frightened stampede of clear shadows. It would long since have melted away in the side turnings had it not been replenished by fresh units surging from mysterious corridors. Tragic, the solitude of those gaunt silhouettes all along the faïence walls before the amorphous cohort opens to swallow them, condemned to the common diktat: *Stop, go! Stop, go!* Dry flesh flapping with the snap of wet linen, grasshoppers stuck in honey, set hopping by a final mainspring—faster, always faster—here you are, as though in the seething poverty of silt, blonde flames, elect bodies! Bruised ivories shadowed with hair, thrice bespattered with night. On top, the little brain motors are still running, spinning tops kept going by the icy whip of fear. Up! Down! Jog! Gallop! *Stop, go! Stop, go!* A shameful troop suddenly disappearing as though swallowed, reemerging to cram itself into the clanging cars of nightmare trains, emerging again more and more maddened, swaying for an instant, shooting forward, then suddenly braking, rising motionless as though in the palm of a gigantic hand that will throw it toward new corridors, new stairways. Faster, still faster. At the mechanical command a meek light appears in the gaze of these damned souls, no doubt a reflection of the feeble heat still retained by their brains along with an awareness of time and place. But that last bit of brightness soon relapses. Thicker and thicker blood beats in their breasts, a panting that merges with the suction of multiple bare feet on stone, in a hissing sound like an animal breathing. This licking, as though welling up from the ground, rises, dies away, returns, hoarse and imperative, swelling until it melts into the automatic murmur flung from the walls of night: *Stop, go! Stop, go!* I no longer ask whether a premonition persists of something that might resemble what yesterday I still called independence, outside me, far from this whirlwind that transports me, terrestrial residue, clamor of hope. Heaped with all the others on the plate of the scales, I await the hour of justice without toga or monocle, justice with a face of concrete. Who are you Fidibus? You aren't Fidibus, you aren't a representative! Who are you? In this night swarming with purple-colored bodies, blackened in this melee of naked Negroes buffeted by the wind, no point in draping yourself in white in order to play at existence, to feign importance in the folds of a shroud. You're no better than those whose black skin merges with the darkness. These tatters to which invisible members still cling with dignity will be swept away one by one.

Through these final swirls of non-being, a dancing light persists and advances. Isn't it another of those treacherous reflective surfaces with which I've collided so often? This time my skull will be cracked forever. No. The black swell in which the crowd has drowned freezes and tightens into a long passage whose walls grow progressively brighter. Soon I make out running toward me a person in a tightrope-walker's costume, dark red tights and a vest whose whiteness seems phosphorescent. All despondency vanishes before the friendly face, the outstretched hands. I'm so happy to escape from a world that I thought beyond remedy that I introduce myself as is customary elsewhere: *Fidibus*. The newcomer giggles, doubtless on account of the comic aspect of these formalities in a corridor where passing would be impossible without clutching each other tightly. He has the agility of an acrobat, but his voice will reveal to us an unusual maturity (that voice, Fidibus, don't you recognize it? Have you completely forgotten everything?). To make up for this disagreeable reflex, he in turn introduces himself, rapidly gripping my hands: *Doctor Three*. In fact, there are now three in front of me. Good lord, these are our fine friends from the Café du Printemps! Pure spirit, there you are flanked by two bodyguards! My good friends, where are you taking me? They no longer have their former air of cunning and brutality. The three of us advance in the wake of the doctor, like soldiers punished with fatigue duty. A door opens on the sill of a huge rotunda. The two simpletons stop, stand to attention, while between them, I stare, bedazzled. Picture a vast, high, circular room of white porcelain, lit up as if in broad daylight by a luminous alabaster ceiling. Everywhere on enamel counters or lacquered tables, strange apparatuses with diamond and mother-of-pearl components. In the middle stands a red marble plinth like a sacrificial table. Standing upright and as though fastened onto this pedestal turned by an invisible pivot, a female silhouette is slowly revolving. Doctor Three, very much at ease in this all-white universe, dons an off-white dressing gown taken from a clothes hook. He looks at the two stationary men framing the doorway: *You see how obedient they are . . .* At these words, I suddenly remember. Just like recognizing a person in a dream (knowing that it's Paul, although he doesn't look at all like Paul, rather like Peter), I recognize the night watchman. It was *Squint* and not *Three* that I should have heard.[5] How can a name be deformed to such an extent? And no doubt this title of Doctor is merely one of his habitual boasts. The little man, puffing smoke from his cigarette, approaches one of the two big lads. Like an automaton, the latter opens his mouth. And now I remember the vile altercation at the Café du Printemps. But, with roles now reversed, it's surpassed in precision and speed by the horror of the scene that plays out before my eyes. The night watchman has casually lifted the hand holding the cigarette and put the glowing end on the patient's tongue. There's only a

MARCEL BÉALU

brief sizzling. The stubbed-out butt is already thrown away, and Squint moves off while, frozen with fear, I follow him. *Why are you trembling, Fidibus? . . . Our friend didn't feel a thing; he's sleeping; when he awakens, a barely perceptible tumor on the tongue, maybe a cancerous tumor . . . Every gob spat into the mouth of a pauper on this here earth must be repaid a hundredfold, no?*

Sure of himself, this diabolical new Squint comes and goes, flapping his white silk sleeves that terminate in two fine strong hands. No trace of the former ragged, filthy Squint save for his speech, swift and full of assurance. It's him, though, yes, it's still the same disturbing individual, but as though cleansed of worldly woes. What had seemed grandiloquent and theatrical in the mouth of the down-and-out has, on the lips of this conjuror, become the natural expression of a reality about which I'm beginning to harbor doubts. Night watchman! Those words, how much new meaning they now possess! I await the revelation of the experiment that he pursues here in this vast laboratory, while the island sinks into nocturnal somnolence. *Have you ever thought that man's one and only sin might have been to have named God too soon—before having realized him? . . .* We've arrived at the center of the room. And once more I recognize, but so close that in raising my arms I can touch her gown, erect in front of me the extraordinary creature whose memory obsesses me. Muta, "she whose life has no purpose." Transformed by her stand, she revolves majestically in a hieratic pose, like a shop-window dummy. Eyelids lowered, her face is immobile below a sort of headscarf wrapped tightly round her temples. Am I dreaming? Am I too alive and dead? My interlocutor's mouth now spouts incredible words, exploding with pride: *Here's my work. The miracle is continually both hidden and evident in this creature to whom I've given human form. If you've found her on the very first day, it's because of all the island you alone were awake, just as you're the only one not asleep in this room ... For everyone else, this woman is nothing more than a silhouette, a dummy. She's alive only for you. Mind you, she still needs several things before attaining the perfection of life ... Alas, the spirit can't do everything, even when assisted by this impressive machinery* (Squint, extending his arm, indicates around him the thousand implements, simple in form but never previously seen that fill me with a mixture of astonishment and fear). *There are certain values that can only be obtained by certain powerful forces—I won't say psychical ones, because I dislike that word, let's simply say love, let's say hate, etc. You should know that I'm counting on you, actually on ... the love that you feel for this creature and that I hope she'll soon feel for you, to endow her with, for example, speech. When her eyes open, they're so close to eloquence. Language! That which refuses, that which says NO in you; your appetite for independence, my dear Fidibus: your curiosity,*

MARCEL BÉALU

your detestable taste for the "newfangled"; everything, everything that the people who live on this island have lost; the mortal impatience that animates you and that can only be satisfied by delirium, waking dreams, laughing fit to die, the solemn night. And I'm absolutely counting on Corinne, on our dear little Corinne's hatred (he carries on in a whisper, so low that I have to strain my ears) *to furnish our chef d'oeuvre with . . . let's say with . . . feelings. Because it's a fact that this pretty lady is entirely devoid of them, capable, if she weren't so soundly asleep on her seat, of the worst acts of cruelty, through pure whim. Ah yes! Give her true nature to her and she'll be ready for the worst excesses . . . like, for example, crushing the bones of a fine young man.*

I wonder if you follow my meaning? Squint continues, reverting to his initial tone of voice. *Here you have the nearly finished sketch of the ideal Being. Just imagine, a compound of the best of everyone, both physically and morally, an amalgam of what's most special in each person, in a word, the prototype of the future race called on to repopulate this island. When I said that she lacks "language" or "feelings," I hope you'll have understood that it was a matter of something else . . . But really, I know that only you, an outsider, and Corinne, still pure, can give our beauty what she in fact lacks. I know that you're the only ones on this island who can represent it.* Represent, representative, represent the representative. All your previous ideas need to be revised, Fidibus. It isn't the past or the future, the professor or the night watchman that you're tasked with re-pre-sent-ing. It's yourself. What differentiates you, what no one will be unless it's you, won't undertake unless you yourself take it in hand. It's what you must endlessly recapture, like molding a figure in soft wax whose features sag as soon as the hand leaves off. It's what won't exist if you don't give it to this thief of "souls," or if he doesn't steal it from you to imbue his monstrous creature. For what is unique in you must become commonplace. You yourself must represent your uniqueness so that everyone can recognize it in themselves. You must lose this most precious good for the benefit of others, because only through losing it will you be delivered, will your inexhaustible obstinacy in justifying yourself be appeased. Fidibus, head in the clouds, Fidibus, little flame capering in the circle of this nameless island, here I am, aware of holding within myself if not the accomplishment of a fantastic future at least a vital part of its accomplishment. But I still don't know its causes or its reasons, neither the why nor the wherefore, just as I don't know whether I'm sleeping, whether I'm dreaming or whether I'm alive. Perhaps I'll be given permission to start life over again in order to finally insert myself completely and unreservedly into the order of things outside myself? The whole past rushes forward as though my life amounted to no more than a minute, and that at the final second—that second on the point of realization—I absolutely had to make up my mind. Ah, why was I left with lucid brain and beating heart? Why hasn't Squint made a puppet of me in the image of the other island dwellers, of those two sleeping servants or of that inert creature on her revolving pedestal? I no longer doubt that it was he who wanted her, fashioned her. What I took for hopelessly muddled verbosity was the manifestation of an imperishable willpower, what seemed to me to be sentimental prattle was the expression of a marvelous, unfathomable reality. The reality that carries the name of silence, the reality that includes dreams and their fleeting impressions, and everything imaginable and unimaginable, and the foreseen and the unforeseen, the bubble on the thick water of the pond and the smooth back of the whale at the rugged surface of the oceans, the fear in the eyes of the newborn baby and the serenity on the brow of the dying man: the reality that also includes what no one has yet seen, what everyone repudiates or is unaware of, what's there, ready to appear in this story, like thunder bursting in the skies above the theater while the beauties of spring are blossoming on the stage.

Squinting and taking small steps back, like an artist inspecting his creation, the night watchman has been silent for a long time. When his voice is once more raised, hesitantly, the impassioned explosion that shook him a short while ago is succeeded by the monotonous recital of the badly paid tour guide. *This rotunda is the island's mechanical brain. The apparatuses it contains only serve the purposes of recording, controlling, adjusting. Everything connects and disconnects at the surface level. You mustn't think either that my powers are unlimited. The game is played without me, I only program the movement, indicate a direction* ... What's the point of these retractions, this reticence so late in the day? I'm only half listening. A line of frosted glass screens claims my attention. Squint pushes a button and one of them depicts a multitude toing and froing amidst a traffic jam. I see Rue des Charmes like a familiar landscape in a dream. But what's that hubbub? The neighboring screen lights up at a second instruction and the smoke-filled and arm-waving room appears. The manipulation of a lever allows the spectator to zoom in or out at will to a specific point. There's the raised platform and the professor flailing his big arms. Finally, his face, and nothing but his face, fills the screen like a big cinematic close-up. *Look*, the voice comments, *the face of a man possessed by the will to power ... at the acme of illusion.* Suddenly I'm aware that this reflection isn't a staged scene but corresponds to reality. The reality of life toward which the churning canal locks of recovery are leading me. *They won't have finished before dawn*, the night watchman mutters, to himself this time. And turning to me: *When you arrived on the island, I saw you through one of these illuminated portholes. You were gazing avidly at a young woman who took off her overcoat, her gloves, her hat. I laughed at your amazement when you saw her disappear in her underwear. If only you'd rushed to follow her! You'd have seen that she modestly put on a white coat and some minutes later, moving like an automaton, took that little iron staircase that you saw down below . . . Yes, Corinne is my only assistant. You see how far off the beaten track the imagination can stray!* But as though he only supplied these explanations so as to voice a concern that was weighing too heavily on him, Squint adds: *What's she doing right now? . . . What's Corinne doing?* These words convey my own thoughts exactly, and when, with feigned detachment, he continues, *Do you want to see another corner of the island? . . . Hold on, there's your room,* we lean together over one of the screens where the room that I thoughtlessly abandoned a short while ago comes into view. With the same degree of attention we both see, enlarged under the action of the zoom switch, the face of the young woman, tense with anxiety and leaning over a prone body. Corinne, pregnant, is alone at the bedside of an invalid, brooding over the two existences imprisoned in the limbos that are separated by immense barren regions. A singular aura of maturity suffuses her face. Unmoving guardian, torn between the two, she listens, first to the life quickening in the thick bush of blood wedged in the thin stem of her waist, then next, outside herself, she tries to grasp the fevered murmur of that other life bearing its spirit into inhuman zones. This double torment gives way to another worry. It seems that another task is urgently calling her somewhere else, one that grows with every passing minute, but to which she decides not to rush hotfoot, decides not to stop listening to the unconscious agitation and the incoherent murmuring mysteriously united in the canal of her ear. It's only when a peaceful sleep overtakes the restless body that Corinne finally makes up her mind to leave it to run toward this former duty, the way you obey a habit, curbed for a moment, but that nothing can make you neglect. The night watchman and I observe this proceeding together. But before rejoining the body that I've now recognized as my own, I'll be the only one to murmur, and in such a manner of voice that the syllables, as though echoed by a thousand trumpets, will erect a multitude of impregnable walls all round me: *My love!*

MARCEL BÉALU

IV

My love ... On opening my eyes, I wonder whether it's really me who has just uttered them, or some vanished presence, those two syllables whose sweetness lingers in the empty room together with their echo. As the memory of my fall comes back to me, I move my limbs with feelings of delight, finding none of them broken. In casting a fresh look around me, a single query floats to my lips from that plunge between life and death: Corinne? Moving hesitantly, I go and sit near the window while waiting for her. The ruptured zinc of the gutter still dangles over the void, and my eye measures the distance separating me from the courtyard flagstones. The Hotel Providence must truly be providential for my fall to have escaped a fatal outcome! And how derisory the price of my recklessness would have been, a vision no sooner glimpsed than gone! Now, at last, all my hopes aspire toward Corinne's more human face, toward the flower of her flesh fecundated by me and ready to bear fruit, toward the blood of my blood, and no longer toward an image that's as though dissipated by the phantasms of my delirium. Who among us has never felt the urge to seize his interlocutor by the shoulders—that friend, that most intimate of friends—and shout at him, *Stop lying!* Someone has certainly shaken me like that, between his two great nocturnal hands. And here I am gripped by a sense of urgency that will end only with the return of Corinne. In my impatience I smile, happily returned to life, happy at the idea of hearing her voice calling me from the stairway, seeing the door open and standing before her, contemplating her face lit up with an expression of joy—Joy! But, coming from the courtyard, it's a shout like an order that I hear, hurried footsteps, then the noise of overturned furniture, a whole bizarre uproar. Are my wits wandering again? Examining the shadow-play below me more intently, I realize that the scene outside has undergone a change. Windows I had seen closed gape open, shutters swinging, as though the human swarms they sheltered had just streamed out from them. What fresh arrival or removal is in progress? Has the Hotel Providence found a buyer, or is a seizure of the property under way? What's happening, or has happened, on the island during that confused period of my recovery? I hear the rumble of a vehicle, the bang of a last shutter, then some words flung like oaths, and once more the sound of running in the dark. At last, everything is quiet. All round me nothing more rises with the darkness save the silence of definitive abandonment.

MARCEL BÉALU

Corinne? Where is Corinne? My uneasiness becomes intolerable. I must tear myself away from this isolation, run in search of Corinne, thrust myself back into the affair that elsewhere, perhaps close by, is taking place without me, unfolding its certainties without me. Feverishly I head for the staircase, descending with awkward but increasingly firm steps. In the midst of my distress, I feel with deep pleasure the new strength of my joints.

An already yellowing little poster on a door announces *For sale to the highest bidder* . . . I don't pause to read any more. This notice posted on every house and the increasing uproar on Rue des Charmes are enough to convince me that the time is out of joint. I approach hurriedly and the hubbub increases. The end of the street is completely blocked by a busy crowd of people and a variety of vehicles: trucks, wagons, handcarts, wheelbarrows etc., which is no small surprise, for these vehicles were hardly to be found on the island before now. What's the meaning of this hullabaloo? While wanting to think of Corinne and nothing else, I must yet again surrender to fresh concerns. The truth is that I can't rub two ideas together, what with all the noise. No sooner have vehicles spilled their contents onto the pavement than they are promptly loaded up on other wagons; a heap of paraphernalia is continually coming and going, coming from who knows where and going to who knows where.

The meeting hall globe glows like a white star above the murky crowd. Inside, where I manage to insinuate myself, the hubbub rivals that on the outside. Through smoke thick as cotton wool, I make out the professor in the distance, waving his big arms while shouts and curses erupt from all around. Near him, behind a table, a man brandishes a mallet. Notwithstanding the disorderly conduct that gives the impression of a gathering of epileptics, what we have here is in fact a massive and hastily conducted auction. The shifting tides of onlookers allow me to gradually approach the platform. Announcing each sale, the professor, a mercenary proclaiming news of a victory, punctuates its conclusion with such savage whoops and yells that his exultation scares me. So keen is he to close deals quickly that he hardly bothers with higher bids. Nevertheless, objects are continually transported here, in such profusion that the session is unlikely to finish anytime soon. Sweat streams down his face and with the noise of each sharp blow of the mallet his jaw is twisted by a nervous tic, a grimace that can hardly be described as a laugh. The sums flung from every corner of the room by so-called buyers are completely unrelated to the real value of the object up for sale. This is nothing but a parody of an auction, an almighty muddle, an unspeakable squandering. I'm also struck by the expression of the assistants, profoundly downcast, as though condemned never to leave the room and as though the grotesque spectacle has been going on for weeks with

MARCEL BÉALU

no end in sight. What does the imperturbable auction-eer lift and shift with swift blows of his tireless mallet? A dusty placard reads: SALE TODAY. But it's nearly mid-night; does it refer to the day now nearly at an end, or another day absent from the calendar, the great day of the final and definitive clearance? Only the smallest items of furniture or easily manageable objects arrive on the platform, trinkets, fabrics, jewelry, heartbreak-ing witnesses of worn-out existences. All this pre-owned stuff emerges from nests of sadness and is passed above heads, from hand to hand, to reach a ridiculous summit. The biggest or heaviest items of furniture are sold, often by lot, on the word of the auctioneer. A continual to-ing and froing between the platform and the low doors cut into the walls is nevertheless necessary. Through these portals all the bric-a-brac that has accumulated over the centuries in the most secret sanctums of the Galeries Ogyges arrives nonstop on the back of laugh-ing porters who exchange coarse greetings. Shortly after my arrival the noise intensifies further, underlining the convulsive character of this sinister bedlam. To top it all, a little mother-of-pearl revolver ends up in the profes-sor's hands, and rather than parting with it he flourishes it, shouting louder than ever, accentuating the blows of the mallet on the table with its pretty little butt. Inspired on the spur of the moment by the batch of bullets that comes with the thing, and to better punctuate each sale, he soon starts to fire off repeated shots, shattering lamps and lampshades, the crystal pendants of chandeliers, the heads or adornments of statues, anything that displays the slightest ambition of rising above the norm.

I flee from these deafening detonations through one of the openings. After a long corridor crowded with porters, I pass through several rooms that I recognize as the ones where no doubt I lost my way yesterday (or how many years ago and in what other world?). These successive depots seem much less cluttered, some of them almost entirely bare. But a number of detours that had escaped my investigations expose other doors to view, revealed by the removal of stacked-up furniture. Pushed open, they enable entry to new galleries that, just like the preceding ones, are crammed from top to bottom. The removal men haven't come to the end of their labors! Cheerful scavengers moving about everywhere, they attack the job of clearance enthusiastically, accompanying the free-for-all with jeers and coarse laughter. Here, two colossi are bent under a groaning wardrobe; there, a grimacing midget carries an ebony Christ that he brandishes feet foremost like a sword. Elsewhere, an adolescent with a plebeian face drags a marble Venus as though it was a corpse, yelling an obscenity at two lads kicking an easy chair upholstered in antique silk. Further on, two wisecracking roughnecks, jiggling a Virgin Mary and a

St. Joseph like puppets, shout as I pass, *objects for the crib, or the moth-eaten myth . . .* Three jokers buttonhole me. Their hands rummage about in a trunk that they've just come across, full of old dolls, and one of them, mimicking the professor with the street-trader's rapid-fire gabble, shouts to the rafters his own trumped-up spiel each time he pulls out a new figure: *Selection of old-age pensioners up on their feet, military postures in spite of some convulsive tremors, indispensable for the family drain!—Sizable lot of self-winding salon buffoons, nineteenth-century style!—Assortment of little ladies of the night, featherlight, adjustable and detachable, heart on hand, ingrown ass, Yankee smell, camping gear, exodus, doomsdays, etc. etc.!* At the bottom of the trunk, the broken or decayed dolls can only be yanked out piecemeal. The three lads toss here a head in the air, there a hand, there a foot, while the increasingly sardonic and flippant voice itemizes mockingly: *Noble figure of imperturbable gravity, totally hollowed out inside, easily portable!—Poet's heart complete with his inkpot controller (bib in good order)!— Barely sketched new smile!—A fine, old, and immutable sorrow, proof against every trial, beware of imitations!— Sly expression, will fit any face, very handy for avoiding conversational embarrassments!—Morals of a great man within reach of every pocket!—Brain from the marrow of an elder tree!—Fresh eyes of dead children for blind octogenarians!—Stale tears, spongy characters, scrapings of conscience* . . . Nothing but debris is coming out of the trunk. I move away, leaving the huckster strangling on his hiccups like a faucet choking under excessive pressure.

I wander from group to group, room to room, losing hope of seeing Corinne amidst this mayhem. Finally, I come across Squint's two partners, stripped to the waist, striving to shift a heavy gothic sideboard whose bulk seems all of a piece with the wall. As they pause to draw breath and wipe away their sweat, one of them notices me. Fear and fatigue must be written on my face. He calls me a *greenhorn*, but in a paternal voice that's less an insult than an invite. *Come and give us a hand, ya wimp!* the other one says. I accept, with the idea of finding out something about the changes taking place on the island. My first question makes them burst out laughing. They seem to be drunk, but with a lucid inebriation whose elation shows on shiny faces with bulging eyes. Their combined effort, for I can't speak of my extremely feeble helping hand, hasn't yet succeeded in budging the wooden monument by as much as an inch, when, by dint of being shaken, the entire facade, doors and door frame, collapses in a cloud of acrid dust, leaving the assemblage of supports that make up the interior partition riveted to the wall. My backward leap must be comical, for one of the two companions, though hit by a fragment of the paneling, can't stop laughing while patting

MARCEL BÉALU

his bloodied forehead with the back of his dirty hand. The other one, a maddened bull by contrast, grabs the sideboard's upright post and using it as a battering ram, charges from one end of the room to the other, attacking the section of sideboard that remains in place. Under the repeated assault, the wood bursts into splinters and finally the structure disintegrates. A door appears in the saltpeter wall, swarming with frightened insects, its upholstering black with mildew. A copper sign that the brute's onslaught has almost wrenched free hangs from a single nail. Our trio of heads, which must surely make a funny-looking group, lean over together to make out the inscription that's still swaying to and fro under the clotted verdigris:

ADMINISTRATIVE COUNCIL

Though we haven't moved a finger, the two sections of the double-leaf door, freed from the monumental sideboard that hid them, open with a slight creak as though pushed from within. We find ourselves on the threshold of a little sitting room whose old-fashioned intimacy contrasts with the disorder and the miscellaneous litter of the rooms that have succumbed to looting. Two old ladies are seated in front of a fireplace. In the middle of this low mantel opening onto darkness, a meager fire, slightly fanned by the draft of our entry, resembles the flickering flame on church altars. I'm as much disconcerted by the indifference of these two females as by the light artfully spilling over the antiquated furnishings. What! Haven't they taken any notice of the uproar at their door? And yet a cupboard yawning open, several rolled-up carpets, the traces on the walls of unhooked pictures, make it clear that they haven't escaped the changes under way, even if paying them little heed. Dressed in threadbare black taffeta now green with age, they're wearing chokers of yellowed lace whose whalebone ribs poke into their sagging chins. One seems younger than the other, although it's impossible to determine their age. The hesitation of the two workmates, then their embarrassment and their suddenly almost deferential faces leave me with the suspicion that the so-called needlework to which the two ladies are devoted possesses the singular virtue of holding in check these two louts (who are hardly deterred by respect for anything whatsoever). Certainly, the two needlewomen getting up at that moment, or even merely pointing to the exit with a little finger, is all it would take to make my two companions—and me too no doubt—run away as fast as our legs could carry us. And the doors themselves would close, preserving this place of sovereign tranquility. And nothing of what's going to happen would happen. Whoever thinks themselves powerless becomes so. Probably resigned to their fate, the two women make not the slightest movement and, recovering quickly from their stunned surprise, my two ruffians go to work, one grabbing a console

MARCEL BÉALU

table, the other ripping the curtains from the window and loading himself up with them. Other workers are already coming in, exiting again with fully laden hands, disappearing in the direction of the saleroom. Still dumbfounded, I remain motionless, eyes fixed on these women who continue their decorative work as though unaware of the encroachment of the outside world. The halo of nobility that floats around their slightly bowed foreheads surprises me less than the atmosphere of that "interior" fitted out in such an exclusive fashion. The quality of such furnishings would have caught my attention in showroom windows or stockrooms no less than in inhabited apartments. Taken by surprise, or because in a few minutes nothing (as I know for sure) will be left of the reasons for my enthusiasm, a question occurs to me: *Where are we?* Graciously, but in a croaking voice, the old woman who seemed absorbed in the production of the fine lace, putting her spindles aside, replies, *Come here young man, don't be afraid . . .* (and placing her wrinkled finger on an imperceptible point of the work spread out in front of her). *Look . . . we're there.* It then dawns on me that these networks of numberless stitches are the map of the island. And a strange thought, analogous to that which seized me on seeing Squint shuffling the cards (a stupefying thought in which I must locate the origin of all this), will suggest to me this time that everything that happened inside this little salon was linked through impalpable correspondences with the slightest events on the outside, and that even the revolution that was upending its harmony wasn't foreign to these skilled hands. The sign on the door reading *Administrative Council* that I thought had been placed there by mistake, suddenly acquires renewed significance.

I'm still caught in the illuminating beam of that thought when the *younger* of the two ladies—can this word be used to designate a mummy like this?—turns and directs her lorgnette toward that part of the room plunged in the shadows. A voice like fritters tossed into boiling oil issues from the wrinkled lips of her rounded mouth: *Brother! Are you still playing with dolls? . . . What color hair have you chosen for your lovely lady?* The object of her address, whose motionless silhouette I hadn't noticed until now, moves toward the feeble light coming from the fireplace. It's Squint. Without replying to the question, he utters my name by way of introduction. I'm grateful to him for giving my actual name rather than the assumed name *Fidibus*, which I'm beginning to find tiresome. Blushing, and perhaps on account of the respectful tone of his voice, I kneel and, one after another, kiss their delicate hands, dry as fish skin. To better see me, one of the venerable ladies tries, with a slight movement, to push aside the white curls at her temples, but slight though it is, this movement disintegrates the fine locks, powdering the black silk of her corsage, revealing a cranium as wrinkled as a coral growth. The croaking voice once more surges from that living skull which nods to me: *My son, is this one here the representative you've told me about?* I don't have to worry about replying, that phrase having been thrown out like a meaningless refrain. The intonation, however, is so remarkable that it sounds like nothing less than the confirmation of the imminent catastrophe. The porters' heavy footsteps return, and, just when one of them with a face as black as a coalman grabs hold of a Louis xv clockface, the first chimes of midnight break loose from it. But as though overpowering a fabulous animal in order to slaughter it, the man smashes the convex crystal with his fist and, with a cracked sound, the music is cut short in a fracas of shattered glass. Sleeves rolled up showing hairy arms, two others approach the women to grab their seats from right under them. They've plunged their noses back in their work and, hardly batting an eyelid, remain suspended, supported only by their little feet on the rim of the andirons. A last removal man, inspecting the room now cleared of its furnishings, must take me, stationary, for some candelabrum for I see him move toward me with one of his helpers. But the night watchman dashes forward: *Stop there*, he cries, *this one here isn't for sale ... Take those two there instead.* Before the ruffians can lean over to carry out the order, Squint, quicker to move, breathes twice on the respectable old women which was all it took for them to crumble, spill, scatter like a cake of ashes. In a few minutes, the room that reflected the cozy wellbeing of secure and luxurious lives has acquired the look of places that have been long abandoned. Damp seeps under the torn wallpaper and the dust floating everywhere seems to come from the hearth where the last ember is dying. Someone has grabbed the lamp and vanished into neighboring galleries, plunging us, Squint and myself, into a twilight gloom verging on darkness. I'm startled when, following a mechanical rattle, the clockface abandoned in a corner emits the last astonishingly pure chimes of the hour that, like a blade, separates the truth of yesterday from that of today. But the night watchman takes my arm to pull me toward a narrow doorway from which projects a rectangle of light.

I immediately recognize the imposing leather armchair, the carpet, the X-shaped seat, and the sarcophagus-like piece of furniture against which *Muta* leaned. I gaze without surprise at the rest of the room into which, for my damnation, I tried so desperately to look. Neither am I surprised by the fact of finding myself here, in the apartment neighboring mine. *Here you are chez moi . . .* Squint says. I take some comfort from the silence that nothing, it seems, is able to disturb. Barely recovered, I'm sunk in such a profound state of lethargy by the weariness of that overlong vigil that my lips can't even form Corinne's name. Is Squint, thinking to respond to my worried look, going to talk to me about *Muta*? And yet, despite everything in this room that evokes her, I would much rather open the windows to see my own room up there. Perhaps Corinne is waiting for me there? But what is it that the night watchman is saying? Do his words express anything other than the confusion of my own thoughts? This is no longer his interminable operatic rant but, finally, clear explanation, precision, the "document": *For a long time you've been trying to find out about this woman and it wasn't possible for me to tell you . . . I admit that I didn't want to introduce her to you in the pathetic condition that's been hers for so long. But you've earned the right to know more, and I'd be truly sorry if you threw yourself out of the window again. Particularly because you probably wouldn't get away with it a second time . . . To come to the point! She, my dear prisoner, the one you call Muta, is the one and only inheritor of the last proprietors of the island. It's thanks to her largesse that each of the inhabitants continues to survive, and the sale of her goods will be a catastrophe for everyone. As you've seen, these benighted souls hurry joyfully to their own downfall! If the professor, less blind than them, sells off an inheritance accumulated over generations at a knockdown price, it's in the hope that the profit will revert to him . . .—But*, I can't keep from interrupting, *why doesn't your . . . friend assert her rights? Why doesn't she put a stop to this sell-off?—For a very simple reason, dear boy: because she's mad. The story's too long to tell and I'll only fill in the main lines for you*, Squint continues, reading the extreme weariness on my face (so extreme that this "very simple reason" which had never occurred to me hardly comes as a surprise). *Kidnapped as a child by the professor's henchmen, Muta grew up in misfortune, even though nature had endowed her with an incomparable beauty. By means of this crime my brother thought he could annul the conditions of a will that thwarted him since the inheritance only passed down the male line in the absence of female heirs. With the child hidden away, we—him and me—should by rights have had an equal share in the property of this district. But soon afterward Corinne was born, so becoming in turn the sole inheritor. The professor didn't dare repeat his nefarious act, but he took advantage of my absence (about this time, having gotten wind of his villainy, I left the district for several years in order to track down the vanished child) to marry my wife and thus officially dispossess me of my daughter. I've never exactly known what he had in mind for her, but the man's history boded nothing good. Happily, you arrived! Without realizing it you've saved her from her stepfather's clutches. And if your child is a girl, this district, its past and its wealth, will end up in her hands . . . For a dilettante you haven't done at all badly!* Squint adds, his irony tempered with affection. What does all this mean? I'm no longer trying to detect implausibility. Little by little my concern with understanding what it is that thrust me into the crowd outside has subsided. The only effort I'm still making is to go on listening. *When I*

MARCEL BÉALU

found Muta again an illness had not only deprived her of her hearing, voice, and hair, but also, as I've told you, her reason. Nothing mattered to me anymore except that creature whose disabilities were eclipsed by her beauty. She became my glory and my shame. Having started out with the intention of revenging myself on the professor by bringing back her whom he believed dead, I was caught in my own trap. Giving up everything in a bid to cure her I became the vagrant you know. I was forced into a thousand lies by our clandestine life on the island where, secretly, I had brought her back ... One evening I made the culpable error of leaving these windows open, never guessing that a passerby would be mad enough to come and live in a condemned hotel ... While I now can't easily grasp the meaning of these words buzzing in my ears, they lift a weight from my shoulders. In my efforts, overwhelmed with fatigue, I must finally have succeeded in pronouncing Corinne's name, for it seemed to me that Squint got to his feet, assuring me that she would soon be by my side.

When I open my eyes, the night watchman is no longer there, but I'm delighted to see that I only need to reach out my hand for a lavish cold repast, served up while I was dozing. I eat ravenously while gazing more attentively at my surroundings. Just as I was struck by the furnishing of the neighboring room on account of the indefinable charm of beautiful things doomed to destruction, so I'm reassured by the nonchalant comfort of the styles in here. In this protected place everything is arranged for relaxation and the delicate pleasures of reverie and the soul. The flames of a wood fire in the fireplace cast a warm and shifting sheen over the hangings. Under the subdued light of two floor lamps the blonde billows of the thick furs that partly cover the floor break against the glowing red tiles of the hearth. With my appetite now satisfied, I seem to see a form stirring amid this downy mass, outlining a silhouette in front of the fireplace. In the light directly reaching her as she turns toward me, I recognize the unfortunate woman whose adventures Squint has just now narrated. What beauty! Is it possible that so much suffering has left not a trace! She's stretched out insouciantly and I'm stunned by her proximity. She's looking at me, yes, that really is the gaze, those are the bright pupils that I've seen in no other woman, those really are the features that have never ceased to haunt me. Muta! It's really her! But all the ambiguity that has surrounded her until now has evaporated, just as almost all her mystery has been dispelled by Squint's confession. How could I have mistaken a bit of ground condemned to redevelopment for the center of the world, and the most banal of human conflicts for a demiurge's fantastic experiment? The fabulous illusion that carried my delirious brain to the height of derangement collapses. The woman before me is nothing more than a poor lunatic who has been held captive by a wretch who is possibly as mad as she is! But much as I might grasp this new set of circumstances and blame my extravagant imagination, I can't dismiss a misgiving; what if my disillusion, resulting from too much clarity, is just as much a part of the program? Perhaps there's only a seeming contradiction between my muddled interpretations and the perfectly lucid ones that the false night watchman is currently foisting on me? Besides, how can I talk about disillusionment when the apparition, hitherto incomplete, has been revealed to me in her absolute perfection, that's to say enhanced by a magnificent head of hair, its refulgence highlighted by the flames from the fireplace? (I should add that the idea of disillusionment stems from that very perfection, from a flawlessness that leaves no room for the realization of my own tastes.) Inasmuch as Squint has succeeded in restoring that embellishment, he'll certainly succeed in recuperating her sanity, her voice and hearing too. But is this necessary? What can be added to such formal perfection? Since the visible has seemingly been achieved here it could not be otherwise with the invisible, as though flesh and spirit defied separation. This is no longer the erect statue in the middle of the laboratory engendered by clouds, but the creature of flesh and blood whose strange gaze held me spellbound. Completed at the crown of her head by this flood of silky purple she truly represents the most tempting of all imaginable creatures, both Eve, first tasked with the fruits of sin, and the supra-terrestrial divinity,

I don't know which, called on by the testimony of her immaculate splendor to preside over the Judgment that will terminate the impersonal human adventure. A few words that I stammer reverberate so inappropriately that I instantly remember how preposterous language is in this place, at this time. That gaze meeting mine, does it not suspend all thought, solve all problems, expressing in a split second everything that's confused in my soul: supreme aberration and supreme awareness. Unable to believe that this smile that enraptures me is uncomprehending, I've approached the madwoman. Dressed in a gown of fine gauze, she remains almost immobile, half extended on the thick furs covering the floor. The heat from the flames scorches my cheeks, or perhaps it's the slight stimulus from the food I've just consumed. Unless, that is, I'm beginning to be stirred by the nearness of these feminine forms visible in all their abundance under the transparent veil. Never was a trap more tempting! If those ears can't hear or that mouth speak, it's evident from these wide-open eyes that I'm seen by them, in an appeal that's more eloquent than any spoken word, never mind that their pupils remain fixed strangely beyond me. Confronted, however, by this body which, on account of an automatic residue of life's ingrained habits, I'm about to despoil, it isn't carnal desire that I feel, but the need for an approach that amounts to a complete identification, whether I am annihilated in it, or it in me.

MARCEL BÉALU

My fingers are mingling with the moving reflection of the flames to caress the birth of this face whose smile fascinates me when a slight tremor of her shoulder, a shiver that seems to convulsively echo the sparkle of her black eyes, makes me examine still more closely the two pupils so strangely fixed beyond me. And suddenly I turn round, raising a stupid brow at Squint, buried in the vast armchair where I hadn't dreamed of suspecting his presence, and who hasn't ceased gazing at Muta. I don't know whether the night watchman is mocking my dismay or registering my shame. But in that final second, the imperceptible irony of his gaze fills me with the certainty that, regardless of his story, nothing has changed, that nothing can change the truth glimpsed in my delirium, and that none of my thoughts, none of my movements, possess any existence outside his will. Once more that conviction penetrates me like a lightning flash, for in the very moment that this inconvenient witness appears before me there's a sound of violent blows and, under their force, the door, bursting free from its hinges, comes crashing down. In its framework, Squint's two men let Corinne through. A frightening Corinne, the bulge of her stomach outthrust, hair disheveled, face dirty, eyes gleaming, and holding between her fingers the little revolver with the mother-of-pearl grips already seen in the professor's hand. The sudden irruption is dominated by three sharp gunshots. Then something occurs of which I will remain the only witness, endlessly questioning its meaning. That Squint was so intimately linked to his creation that no shot could be aimed at her without first hitting him, that much I was prepared to admit. But this brutal resurrection of a soul—or of a body . . . what do I know?—this utter annihilation of a divine or demonic power, wasn't it the price paid by his imperturbable cruelty? The overreaching of norms that Squint had sought in fabricating a kind of ideal monster made up of the best of everyone with no concern for the human waste that would be entailed by such a puncturing of the essential, this transgression was no less cruel than the promiscuity desired by the professor, was perhaps more so. At that moment the human waste—the unused, the dead wood—took its revenge. Corinne, without seeing the night watchman still concealed by the back of the armchair, fired at Muta. Her tense little finger was pulled scarcely two meters from that target, perhaps, like me, frozen by the unexpected. And yet it's the night watchman who hasn't made a move and so, I repeat, remains unseen by the killer, it's Squint I say, who collapses, hit by the bullets, while Muta (or to be more exact, that which goes by that name) stands up as though suddenly liberated. Everything that composed the majesty of her allure vanishes, her eyes, losing their serenity, are full of furious movement, her face, as though grimacing, transforms into a different face. A cry, a stammer of atrocious fury comes from her lips. It's no longer Muta whom Corinne and I see before our eyes; we recognize Beatrice.

MARCEL BÉALU

A lost Beatrice, mad, surging distractedly from a long sleep. Before I can recover from my stupor, that maenad, half-naked, breasts bared, bends down, seizes a burning log and, wielding the improvised torch, followed by the two men, rushes at a wild pace through the floors where the crowd is now abandoning itself to pillage.

Corinne, as though she too has awoken, seeing her mother before her instead of the rival she thought she'd shot, thinks she's blundered. Having thrown away her weapon she casts frightened looks all around. Despite her confusion, I try to tell her about the transformation I've just witnessed, trying myself to comprehend the mystery by putting it into words. But before I can grab her arms and embrace the trembling rebel, she's flung herself after Beatrice. Recovering my wits, and not without a last glance at Squint, doubled up on the seat of the chair, I launch myself in pursuit. My hesitation has allowed the girl a head start. *Corinne! Corinne!* I shout at the top of my lungs. The further away we get from the chaotic rooms the more I'm assailed by the fear, then the terror, that she's in the grip of a desperate resolve. Stairs, corridors, newly emptied storerooms echo my call. Arriving at Rue des Charmes, and still hindered by the throng of noisy groups, I make out a white silhouette rushing unhesitatingly toward the narrow defile that descends to the embankments. When I succeed in freeing myself, she's increased her lead, but I'm spurred on by the hope of gaining on her before she reaches the river. Panting, I run without pausing to catch my breath. The passersby who don't get out of my way quickly enough are knocked aside, shoved into shadows already thick with curses. Gradually it's only the sound of my running that hammers the silence, clinging to the distant vision of Corinne who is lent wings by the folds of her blouse and who seems to fly, a pale, dancing brightness appearing, disappearing, always further ahead. At one point I think I've caught her. Begging, *Corinne, Corinne!* . . . I see her stumble some twenty paces from me, weighed down by the burden of her expectant belly. It seems to me that she slows, hesitates, finally hears me. Then, abruptly, she disappears. I discern a fall into the water, a confused disturbance at the black surface. I dive in. How long afterward was it that I found myself seated beside a corpse on the grass of the bank, more than two hundred meters further on? I remember having swum for a long time, diving tirelessly, searching gropingly in the dense river, my open fingers gripping aquatic plants or rotten trunks, and each time my heart leaping with an increasingly desperate hope. Finally, carried by the current, I almost collided with her for whom I was searching at an overflow outlet, held under the surface by her hair caught in the branches. Laboriously, I managed to pull her up onto the riverbank and for a long time worked desperately on her body, trying to resuscitate her, imploring the aid of the divine powers. Now, dazed, I touch an ice-cold stomach, her entrails a prison wherein rests the perpetuation of my own existence. Is it for this receptacle from which life has scarcely fled, or for the other life that I'll never know, a corpse inside a corpse, or is it for my own life that, fitfully, rising abruptly to my feet, I persistently call out, shouting for help? But what help can I expect on this calamitous island surrendered to madness? The slight rustling of leaves disturbed by the current invariably ends up drowning out my calls. When will the day break? A pink reflection lies on Corinne's little forehead, like a leaf of mother-of-pearl. But this is merely the distant reflection of gleams of light that are now rising high behind me. All the upper district of the island is aflame. The inferno of this accursed district, will it rise high enough to set the sky alight? *Corinne! . . . Look! . . . It's over, I'm cured, we can go away, our child will be born. Everything is saved.* I rave, once more delirious, under the false daylight of the fire, holding the fragile body, already rigid, in a tight embrace. Fiery sparks, lifted by the virulence of the blaze and carried on the wind, fall around us, on us. *Us! . . .* I'm alone once again, numb to the rain of sparks, with my ice-cold embrace as my sole recourse. When a crumb of reason returns, the sun, already high, illuminates a heap of blackened debris above the district's shanties. Even the sand, tarnished, soiled, has lost its blonde complexion. Corinne and I are covered with ashes. Only the river remains pure, the water that never stops flowing. In a sudden and perhaps cowardly resolution I take her over to the bank, dragging the double burden with which will perish all my feelings of tenderness, and, in a final effort, give this body, with its now unbearable immobility, to the element that has already stolen its life from me. No doubt I'm hastening the decay of her flesh. Carried off in a few seconds, she disappears in the bosom of a turbulent current. Dear God! may nothing stop her ahead of the shore where your ocean will cast up her bones!

One last time I run through streets where nothing reigns but ruin and abandonment. The entire population appears to have fled. Miraculously intact objects of every kind, escaped from gutted bundles, lie amidst blackened rubble and beams reduced to cinders. Streets and pavements are littered with handcarts that, at the moment of departure, have collapsed under the weight. But as I make my way back up to the center of the island, men and women reappear little by little, emerging from cellars and sections of wall, empty-handed shades that, like me, head in the direction of the bridges. Soon, mingling with a silent crowd gathered with a single purpose that I haven't yet divined, I manage to piece the events together through listening to conversations exchanged in low voices. The professor, instigator of the disorder, has perished along with Beatrice in the blaze that she lit. It isn't known which one dragged the other to that horrifying end. Squint? The memory comes back to me of having left him in the hollow of the armchair in the room next to mine, most likely dead. And nothing is left of the Hotel Providence but smoking walls. When I reach the avenue, I'm carried by the movement of the crowd to the front of some kind of procession that proceeds between the ruins toward the threshold of the bridge. It takes me a long time to realize that in fact the night watchman's remains are borne on it. The emotion of those around me proves that a profound reversal took place after the professor's death. What tremendous return of awareness has swept them up in this sudden devotion toward one whom they considered as the lowest of them all? The hastily knocked-together coffin of four planks has been placed atop a curious hearse: a carriage that is gilded all over, probably the only antique to have escaped destruction. Squint, the ragged tramp, the vagrant, perched between the four red plumes of this anachronistic vehicle! A carthorse, undoubtedly borrowed from the riverside settlements, slowly hauls it along. A crowd mills around the harness in an incongruous medley of clothing, often tattered or flung on at a moment's notice, and with faces that variously express austere pride or excessive humility. But an unfeigned fervor holds them all in its embrace. The swaying, creaking carriage forges a passage through the crowd's currents. The front ranks step respectfully aside, resisting the pushing of the others.

All these people want to get close, touch the vehicle, lift their hands to the plumes, want the chance of bearing subsequent witness to the incredible event, to its tiniest detail even. When the horse, with its heavy, faithful tread, reaches the entry to the bridge, the mob, as though under orders, rushes forward and, unstrapping the harness, besieges the high wheels to take possession of the casket. From afar, I recognize the two men who dispute the honor of shouldering, above the heads, the funeral burden.

1945–1949

TRANSLATOR'S AFTERWORD
THE *BENITO CERENO* KNOT

The Impersonal Adventure went through three different editions in Béalu's lifetime, each with variant texts. The first 1954 edition was published by Eric Losfeld in his Collection Arcanes. In 1970, Éditions Gérard reissued the novella parceled up with a number of Béalu's short stories in their mass-market Marabout Fantastique series. This edition made some minor textual changes, corrected a few typographical errors and imported the Arcanes list of section titles directly into the text, so as to act as section headings. Then, in the definitive edition published by Phébus in 1985, Béalu returned to the formal arrangement of the 1954 edition, with section titles listed separately. He also made one further addition, namely a lengthy epigraph taken (in French translation) from Herman Melville's novella *Benito Cereno*. The epigraph concerns a sailor's knot so complex as to be inextricable:

> Captain Delano crossed over to him, and stood in silence surveying the knot. . . . For intricacy such a knot he had never seen in an American ship, or indeed any other. The old man looked

like an Egyptian priest, making Gordian knots for the temple of Ammon. The knot seemed a combination of double-bowline-knot, treble-crown-knot, back-handed-well-knot, knot-in-and-out-knot, and jamming-knot.

At last, puzzled to comprehend the meaning of such a knot, Captain Delano addressed the knotter:—

"What are you knotting there, my man?"

"The knot," was the brief reply, without looking up.

"So it seems; but what is it for?"

"For some one else to undo," muttered back the old man, plying his fingers harder than ever, the knot being now nearly completed.

Clearly the epigraph was meaningful for Béalu, but its relationship with *L'Aventure* isn't at all obvious; it would seem to function primarily as a provocation intended for the reader—here's a heterogeneously knotted tale, see what you can make of it. I believe, however, that the epigraph is more closely linked to Béalu's narrative than might first appear.

*

> You with your great interest in dreams, have you ever been seduced by Freud?
>
> Certainly. I've read Freud. *The Interpretation of Dreams*, of course.[1]

With the rise to prominence of Jacques Lacan and his epigones, a wave of psychoanalytic theory and a corresponding haute bourgeoise vogue for psychoanalysis infiltrated French culture. Béalu, whose second wife, the actor Marie-Ange Dutheil, underwent a course of psychoanalysis that lasted several years, remained skeptical. He seems to have preferred Jungian psychology, but he was also well aware of surrealism's flirtation with Freud and never lost his respect for the founder of psychoanalysis; he occasionally, if ironically, employed some of its jargon.[2] This perhaps gives me some license to explore a little further the potential relevance of Freudian theory vis-à-vis *The Impersonal Adventure*.

Béalu's refusal of realism in his novella does not mean that the narrative is able to freely indulge in an abusive irrationality that might be justified only as joke or provocation. The fantastic possesses its own rationale, far different, evidently, from everyday experience but not without its own modes of coherence. At a crux point in the novella's final section, however, the irrational erupts in a manner that defies the ability of both narrator and reader to comprehend what has occurred as anything other than a confounding lapse into the nonsensical.

When a heavily pregnant Corinne shoots Muta at point blank range she finds that instead she has, impossibly, killed the night watchman, her father. At the same time, Muta, unharmed by the bullets, is inexplicably transformed into a maddened Béatrice.

We might broach this narrative aporia—this narrative knot—by noting that both the dislocation and the transformation that it entails are characteristic of the methodology that Freud proposed for an analysis of the dreamwork, that is, the processes of displacement and condensation.[3] The shots fired at Muta that instead kill the night watchman correspond to displacement, while Muta's transformation into Béatrice corresponds to condensation. Through these processes, an "unconscious" phantasy may be glimpsed: the Oedipal father is killed and the frenzied mother—a half-naked maenad—is unleashed.

Freud's analysis of his dream of "Irma's injection" in *The Inter-pretation of Dreams*, the inaugural dream of psychoanalytic theory, includes an intriguing footnote: "There is at least one spot in every dream at which it is unplumbable, a navel as it were, that is its point of contact with the unknown."[4] The metaphor of the navel recurs subsequently in a somewhat fuller passage:

> There is often a passage even in the most thoroughly interpreted dream which has to be left obscure; this is because we become aware during the work of interpretation that at that point there is a tangle of dream thoughts which cannot be unraveled. . . . This is the dream's navel, the spot where it reaches down to the unknown.[5]

Freud's "tangle which cannot be unraveled" is the marker of an umbili-cal connection, something that has elicited a good deal of subsequent commentary and analysis, with all agreeing that it implicates a con-nection with the female-maternal dimension:

> Just as the navel describes a knot of meaning that resists full in-terpretation, so Irma's symptoms signal knots that silently refuse psychoanalytic treatment. Feminine sexual difference further-more marks the limits of psychoanalysis's knowledge, the point and object at which psychoanalysis falters. The navel embodies this difference; a scar of one's lost connection to another body, a body that is always female.[6]

It isn't, then, entirely illogical that the inextricable knot in Béalu's nar-rative, which we might tentatively call the *Benito Cereno* knot, should result in the death of a father who has just "finally" supplied "a clear explanation" to Fidibus, while at the same time resulting in the resurgence of the mother as a primitive body outside language ("A cry, a stammer of atrocious fury comes from her lips . . .").

For much of *The Adventure*, Fidibus is attracted to women who are invested with a doll-like status. Corinne sets up and clothes a dummy in her own likeness, and subsequently Fidibus mistakes her for the same dummy. Muta, for her part, becomes for the narrator both an unattainable object of desire and the ultimate, transcendental commodity prefigured by the shop-window mannequins that he sees in the Ogyges window displays and that he initially mistakes for living beings. Throughout the text, Muta's status as an animated doll or mannequin is either implied or directly stated: "she revolves majestically in a hieratic pose, like a shop-window dummy"; "*Brother! Are you still playing with dolls? . . . What color hair have you chosen for your lovely lady?*" As such she follows in the footsteps of a line of fatally seductive female automatons extending from Olympia in E. T. A. Hoffmann's "Sandman" to the robot of Fritz Lang's *Metropolis* (there are passages in *The Adventure* that recall images in Lang's film). This lineage, produced by controlling "fathers," is unnatural and antimaternal in character. Beautiful as she is, Muta, according to Squint, is dangerous: "*It's a fact that this pretty lady is entirely devoid of [feelings], capable, if she weren't asleep on her seat, of the worst acts of cruelty, through pure whim.*"

Born as she is from the scientist-father, from a brain, not body, does Muta possess a navel? Is she capable of pregnancy? Fidibus intuitively understands that she is something more or less than human and this accounts for his fascination with her. In Part II, conversely, he is horrified to learn that Corrine is pregnant with his child—she effectively ceases to be his living doll. For as long as he remains under the spell of Muta, Fidibus repudiates the notion of fatherhood, and in Part II, he turns away from the pregnant Corinne to resume his search for Muta. Only when that spell is finally broken does his desire for the flesh and blood woman return: "Now, at last, all my hopes aspire toward Corinne's more human face." Her pregnancy is now accepted by him—too late.

Corinne's attempted shooting of Muta can be understood in the light of two contrasted images of womanhood: maternal versus fetishized. If we understand Muta as Squint's male fantasy made flesh, then it's intuitively appropriate that the bullet aimed at her in fact destroys her creator, the true object of female-maternal rage. As for Muta's transformation into Béatrice, we might suggest that beneath the male fantasy of the fetishized doll-woman persists the repressed figure of the pre-Oedipal mother, that is, in Freud's view, the phallic mother.

This is a speculative and no doubt dubious reading; nevertheless, it seems clear that with the gunshot and its aftermath, the women take their revenge on the controlling fathers: the night watchman and the professor are killed by, respectively, Corinne and Beatrice, both bearing weapons (a revolver and a burning log, respectively). Corinne then flees from Fidibus and fatally denies his chance of fatherhood.

Did Béalu, in reading *The Interpretation of Dreams*, register Freud's "unplumbable navel"? Further, did he take this "knot" into account in considering his own novella? The question is of course moot, but I would argue that, in any event, the Melville passage involving the inextricable knot can be seen as a forerunner of Freud's umbilical knot—the knot of an unresolvable meaning—and that if Béalu didn't see the connection, he possessed a poet's intuition.

Muta, mysterious and unspeaking, is a screen onto which Squint and Snot, night watchman and professor, project a succession of identities: a beautiful madwoman, a defrauded heiress, a fatal automaton, a tribal goddess of transmutations. For Fidibus she is equivalent to the

Benito Cereno knot which defies undoing. By extension she is also equivalent to the unfathomable node or knot of Freud's Irma dream that seals off an ultimate secret. The psychoanalyst and writer Guy Rosolato would see Muta as an embodiment of what, following Freud's metaphor, he calls *la relation d'inconnu*—a relationship with the unknowable, more specifically a relationship with a female-maternal dimension that escapes (patriarchal) knowing.[7] Thus she remains the novella's ultimate, unfathomable enigma.

One further incidental piece of evidence suggests that in writing *The Impersonal Adventure* Béalu sought to contrive challenging complexities. My copy of the 1954 edition is one that Béalu inscribed to a friend: "Pour L.-G. B. [. . .] ce roman en forme de labyrinthe"—"this novel in the form of a labyrinth."

Attempts to thread a way through some of the labyrinth's intricacies must stop here. My reading of Béalu suggests that he would have greeted the interpretations set out above with an indulgent if skeptical smile, which, I hope, will be the skeptical reader's response too. I have certainly not sought to "explain" the story, which retains all its tantalizing strangeness and mystery—and remains no less knotted than before. The last word can safely be left with the author:

> The writer's only role is to enchant the world and not to disenchant it, to build it rather than to destroy it. . . . The fantastic is the premonition of the supernatural, but it's also the perception of a deeper reality, the premonition, in a word, of surreality. Exactly like poetry. A realism without limits.[8]

NOTES

THE IMPERSONAL ADVENTURE

1. Statues, evidently. Velleda was the first-century female prophetess who foretold the victory of a Germanic tribe over the Romans. Her figure gained new currency in the nineteenth century when she was the subject of novels, an opera, a painting, and a sculpture. I've been unable to identify the "laughing warrior" reference.

2. The French text involves a pun which is lost in translation; the literal meaning of the phrase "creuser son trou" (dig one's hole) is doubled by a colloquial meaning—to find one's place, or to make one's way.

3. "A fidibus is a resin-rich wood chip or a folded strip of paper that serves ... especially for lighting pipe tobacco. The etymology of the term, which emerged in the late seventeenth century, is unknown" (Wikipedia).

4. *Torve* and *Morve* in French. *Torve*, meaning menacing or crooked, often used to convey a nasty look ("oeil torve"), is translated here as Squint; *Morve*, literally "snot," is translated here as "Snot."

5. *Torve* and *Trois* in French.

AFTERWORD

1. Marcel Béalu, *Le regard oblique: Entretiens avec Marie-France Azar* (Paris: Jean-Michel Laplace, 1993), 77.

2. In *Le regard oblique* Béalu referred to his memoirs as an "auto-psycho-analysis," involving the remembering of "forgotten lives" (95). It might also

be worth noting that in 1985 Béalu published a short supernatural tale, *La mort à Benidorm* [Death in Benidorm] (Périgeux: Pierre Fanlac); it seems to me that this owes a debt to Wilhelm Jensen's *Gradiva*, which Béalu, like many others, came to by way of Freud's well-known study of the work. See *Le regard oblique*, 77.

3. See Freud, *The Interpretation of Dreams*, trans. James Strachey (London: George Allen & Unwin, 1982), chapter 6, 279–310.

4. *The Interpretation of Dreams*, 111, n. 1.

5. *The Interpretation of Dreams*, 525.

6. Fred Botting, *Sex, Machines and Navels* (Manchester: Manchester University Press, 1999), 24. See also Didier Anzieu, *Freud's Self Analysis*, trans. Peter Graham (London: Chatto and Windus, 1986), 153; Guy Rosolato, "L'ombilic et la relation d'inconnu," in *La relation d'inconnu* (Paris: Gallimard, 1978); Shoshana Felman, "Postal Survival, or The Question of the Navel," *Yale French Studies* 69 (1985): 49–72.

7. See Rosolato, *La relation d'inconnu*, 270.

8. Béalu, *Porte ouverte sur la rue*, 182–183.

THE SCHOOL OF THE STRANGE

1. *Spells*, Michel de Ghelderode

2. *Whiskey Tales*, Jean Ray

3. *Cruise of Shadows: Haunted Stories of Land and Sea*, Jean Ray

4. *Waystations of the Deep Night*, Marcel Brion

5. *The Great Nocturnal: Tales of Dread*, Jean Ray

6. *Circles of Dread*, Jean Ray

7. *Malpertuis*, Jean Ray

8. *The Impersonal Adventure*, Marcel Béalu